I0640503

SHOES ON A WIRE

by

C. D. Neill

Grosvenor House
Publishing Limited

All rights reserved
Copyright © C. D. Neill, 2020

The right of C. D. Neill to be identified as the author of this
work has been asserted in accordance with Section 78
of the Copyright, Designs and Patents Act 1988

The book cover is copyright to C. D. Neill

This book is published by
Grosvenor House Publishing Ltd
Link House
140 The Broadway, Tolworth, Surrey, KT6 7HT.
www.grosvenorhousepublishing.co.uk

This book is sold subject to the conditions that it shall not, by way of
trade or otherwise, be lent, resold, hired out or otherwise circulated
without the author's or publisher's prior consent in any form of binding or
cover other than that in which it is published and
without a similar condition including this condition being imposed
on the subsequent purchaser.

This book is a work of fiction. Any resemblance to
people or events, past or present, is purely coincidental.

A CIP record for this book
is available from the British Library

ISBN 978-1-83975-042-7

Other books featuring Detective Inspector Wallace Hammond:
Doors without Numbers

****

This book is dedicated to my family, without whom I would be a lost soul. X

"We die ourselves a little every time we kill in others something that deserved to live."

Oscar Hammling (1890-) Laconics

PROLOGUE

The ant's frantic movements as it zigzagged its way past obstacles of gravel did not suggest a state of panic any different from the usual movements of an ant commuting, but to the young man watching it, its pace indicated a creature experiencing the initial phase of crisis. He had been watching the creature for several moments. Occasionally, he had deliberately placed additional obstacles in the path of his interest; a stone, a lump of mud. Sometimes his foot, although he took deliberate care not to press down too hard. He wanted to give the ant a chance to find a furrow in the tread of his training shoe and allow passage. How long he was immersed in his observation he could not calculate. From the moment he had sat down overlooking the docks, time had ceased to exist, despite the constant drone of traffic heading into and out of Dover Town just over a mile away, and the frequent tannoy announcements informing ferry passengers to remain in their cars whilst safety checks commenced.

He lip-synched the words spoken by the voice over the loudspeaker, first in English, then in French, and finally German. English was his first and last language, yet he echoed the diction of the alternative languages perfectly. His familiarity with the sound was partly due to having sat in this place daily for several months and memorizing each word, and partly from the immersion of sound that reverberated off the cliffs and lodged itself into his subconscious. The loudspeaker and general bustle of the ferry terminal were loud enough to be heard a distance away, but the young man remained immersed in his observation of the ant.

He was oblivious to the muffled whimpers that came from inside the van parked several feet away, nor did he notice the squeak as the vehicle rocked on its suspension caused by the panicked movements of the prisoners inside. Even if he had been aware of the activity, he would not have been disturbed from his deliberations. This was his sanctuary, his chosen place.

Eventually, the young man lifted his head, disturbed by an airborne seagull that had swooped low and excreted, narrowly missing his head. Cursing under his breath, he began to stand up, one hand stroking his shaved head to check there was no filthy residue. Now he had forgotten all about the ant. His hand paused above the nape of his neck, his fingers lingering on the St. George's Cross tattoo that covered the back of his skull. He couldn't see it, but it was enough to know it was there. The skin was pimply from the stunted hair that wanted to push through the skin.

The rising warmth from the early August morning sun threatened to burn his exposed head, as it did frequently. His fair complexion made him extra sensitive to nature's elements, but he resisted pulling the hood of his sweatshirt over his head. He wanted the world to see his dedication to his country. His hand returned to his brow to shield his eyes from the sunlight that reflected from the water onto the white cliffs upon which he now stood.

He remained in position, his attention momentarily distracted by the sight of the lorries below him slowly being swallowed by the ferry they were embarking. Amongst the humdrum of noise, he heard the faint bleating of livestock beginning their journey to France. He wondered whether the animals were simply protesting their mere discomfort, squashed together as live cargo, or whether their utterances were those of the desperate and condemned. The sound elated him, the emotion so intense that it threatened to burst from within him. He was inspired by the courage of the inferior who were anticipating their own slaughter. The thought reminded him of his task, and he turned his attention back to the van.

He swiveled round on the heels of his trainers and turned left, back towards the main footpath. The chalk track was smooth underfoot so his venture towards the vehicle was quiet. He stopped at the back of the van, his hands gripping the key for a second before unlocking and opening the doors. The hinges co-operated reluctantly with low groans and allowed him to look inside. His eyes took several seconds to adjust from the sunlight outside, but eventually his sight focused on the huddle of the four passengers. They were bound to one another, yet their clutching at each other's bodies looked voluntary, seeking comfort and strength as one entity. With their arms restrained, they could not shield their eyes from the interrupting glare that entered the darkened van, so they squeezed their eyes closed. They looked pathetic. They stank of unwashed bodies, stale urine and fear.

The young man surveyed them in silence and then spat into the van, causing residue saliva to dribble over his chin stubble. He wiped his chin clean using a cuff of his sweatshirt and slammed the doors shut with exaggerated force. Then he sat himself in the driver's seat. He turned the ignition, allowing the van's engine to idle whilst he selected a track on the audio player. Within seconds, the first strings encouraged a crescendo of chorus to which he joined in, singing as loud as he could. He sang the words with heartfelt passion and purpose, dedicating himself to the country that he was willing to die for, willing to kill for. He pledged his loyalty to the land of hope and glory, his homeland, the mother of the free.

As the van gravitated its way over loose gravel, heading towards the main road, the sounds of the terminal below mingled with the drift of chorus floating through the air as one man sang to his Queen and to his God. The God who had made him mighty and who would make him mightier yet.

*

The young woman who had jogged along the chalk path every day had changed her route since noticing the skinhead who sat on the cliff path. For several years she had run the same route, starting from the White Cliffs Visitor Centre, heading east onto the coastal path. After ten minutes sprint, she would stop at the remains of the Military Prison and stretch her muscles, watching the port below. Then she would switch on her iPod, attach the earpieces, and begin a steady jog, keeping to the path towards Langdon Hole with the sea on her right. On a clear day it was possible to see the 20-mile stretch across the Channel to the French coast. On windy days she kept her head down, struggling against the breeze.

Wooden steps took her onto the flat area of grasslands, and occasionally she would stop here, hoping to see the Peregrine Falcons that nested on the cliffs. But on days when she wanted to test her stamina, she would continue on at a faster pace, following the lower cliff path. When her legs began to tire, she would ignore the sea views now on her left, and pretend not to notice the steep drop as the path narrowed. Instead, she concentrated on the view of Dover Castle nestled amongst the hills straight ahead, and then she would take a sharp turn at the turnstile, back onto the dirt track that was woven amongst trees and undergrowth.

It was near this spot where she had first seen him. Her head had been bent down as she ran, avoiding the lower branches that snagged her elbows. As she had exited the tunnel of overgrowth, she had seen a figure crouched down on the side of the path. He was absolutely still and did not acknowledge her as she passed. From that day on, he was there, always at the same place. And he ignored her every time, which she thought was rather odd. People she came across on her run would normally greet her with a smile or a word of encouragement, some stepping onto the side of the path to allow her passage. But although he never approached her or had given her any reason to be anxious, there was something about the way he stared out at sea without moving.

At first, she thought he was shy, but after several passings she accepted him as being rude. After two weeks, she felt slightly un-nerved and decided to avoid the path altogether, not turning at the turnstile but continuing straight ahead. She didn't like this alternative, because it was a steeper climb near the end, and meant she could not sprint the last few metres the way she liked to do before easing to a stop.

She mentioned her frustration to her boyfriend, Jules, who offered to accompany her and had then seen the man for himself. He had agreed the stranger's behaviour was odd and advised her to avoid her usual route. It was possible the man was a stalker, wanted by the police, or had absconded from a hospital psychiatric ward. There were so many odd characters in Dover lately, the majority suspected to be suffering from drug-induced psychosis, that it was better to be vigilant.

The young woman and the skinhead continued to avoid each other for several months until something happened which aroused her suspicions even further.

It was a calm early morning in August; there wasn't a cloud in the sky; the sea was almost motionless. She felt the urge to pause above the ports and watch a ferry maneuver into one of the docking stations. Despite its cumbersome shape and dimensions, its entry into the docks was graceful enough to impress her and retain her attention for several minutes. Then she heard music and turned to hear where it was coming from. It sounded as if there was an Elgar concert happening at the top of the cliffs, which was odd and out of place, especially so early in the day.

Curious, she followed the sound towards the western approach path. The music intensified as she climbed up the bank towards a clearing and then stopped dead. She saw the skinhead driving towards her in a white van, seeming animated. His hand mimicked a conductor's baton with his right arm hanging out the open window. Instinctively, she crouched down onto her haunches until he passed, not wanting him to see her, and stayed in that position as the van disappeared, the sound of music fading into the distance.

CHAPTER ONE

The call to the emergency line based at Maidstone Head-
quarters was answered at 7am by a switchboard operator just
beginning her shift. It was immediately apparent that the
caller was in distress. The voice at the other end was garbled
and high pitched, the gender unrecognizable.

"I think I have done something awful... Oh God..."

"Could you tell me your name, please?"

"Oh God... Oh God, what have I done? I didn't know
what it was... I didn't have time to stop..."

"Please calm down and tell me your name."

After several seconds, the information flooded through as if
the caller had suddenly realised the reality of their situation.

"My name is David... David Hargreaves... I'm on the side
of the road, on the A20 Ashford bound..." The voice stopped
mid-sentence.

"Can you tell me what has happened, David?"

There was a long pause. "I've driven over someone... I
think I have killed a..." There was a sob. "...I have killed a
child."

Within a few minutes of the call being made, paramedics from
the nearby ambulance station and police officers arrived at the
scene. The officers, who were about to finish their shift within
the hour, knew only that there was a possible fatality of a
minor, following a traffic accident. With almost eighteen years
of experience between them, they had witnessed the aftermath
of traffic accidents before. Some accidents had been forgettable,

others not so; the images of torn bodies and twisted carnage had preoccupied many of their waking moments, but this was an incident that neither officer had been expecting.

A black Mercedes was parked at the roadside. In front of the car on the ground was seated a man dressed in a blue shirt, his face ashen despite the daylight that was already seeping into the day, his eyes wide with confusion. His legs were bent at the knee, his hands curled around his limbs.

"Was it you who called?" The elder of the two officers bent down, placing a firm but reassuring hand on the man's shoulder.

Behind him, the paramedics were occupied with a small bundle in the road. The younger officer watched them, his stare concentrating on their movements. He tried to gauge from their body language whether they were dealing with a fatality, but all he could see was medical equipment being passed in a flurry of activity. His eyes returned to the man who had confirmed he had made the call.

"Ok, David, I need you to tell me what has happened."

The man gulped, his eyes focused on the officer bent down towards him. "I was driving to Ashford. I needed to get to the office early. I have a meeting to prepare for..." He paused, realizing he was digressing. "I turned off from Sellindge and stopped at the give-way by the railway bridge to make way for a white van. It must have been speeding, because it stayed quite a way in front of me... Anyway, I was keeping to the 40 limit... the speed cameras..."

"It's alright, David, We are not apportioning blame yet, we just need to know what happened."

"Yes, of course. I came round the bend just here and the van was quite a way in front of me, but it looked as if the back doors had swung open. I couldn't really see that well, but I slowed down, thinking I should flash the driver to warn him. Then I noticed something in the road." The man covered his eyes as if to block the memory of what he was describing.

"I couldn't stop in time; it was so small and I hit it. I looked in my rear-view mirror. At first, I thought it was an animal, so

I stopped the car to check…" He trailed off mid-sentence. His finger pointed towards where the paramedics were occupied.

One of the paramedics was gesturing for the officers' attention. As they walked over, the female paramedic partially blocked their approach. "It's a fatality." She paused, her eyes avoided their gaze. "I wasn't expecting this."

Confused by her comment, their eyes were drawn to the bundle in the road. The younger officer crouched down and gently eased the covering to reveal the body underneath.

"Jeez…" He stopped. His eyes registered the greasy, waxy surface of translucent skin, blue swollen limbs; the battered head looked out of proportion to the rest of the body. The tiny hands clasped together with the intricate webbing of newly-formed fingers. The eyes tightly closed. The mouth still open; a newborn's first cry permanently silenced.

*

Detective Inspector Wallace Hammond popped the remainder of the cereal bar into his mouth before stuffing the wrapper in his trouser pocket. A quick glance in the car's rear-view mirror assured him there were no tell-tale crumbs caught on his chin bristle. Self-consciously, he ran his hand over his face and wished he had shaved that morning. Hopefully, no-one would notice.

He took the key out the ignition and got out, before turning his attention to DS Lois Dunn.

"We need to tread carefully with this one. Apparently, the guy was in shock when he was first questioned, so we need to let him do as much talking as possible. That way, we won't be seen to be insensitive but will still be able to spot any inconsistencies with his story."

Dunn looked at him from over the roof of the car. "You think he has something to hide?" She was wearing patent shoes with a higher heel than usual protocol allowed.

As he stepped around the back of the car, depressing the lock button on the car key fob, Hammond made a mental note not to stand at her side during the introduction. He had to look as if he was the one in charge.

He shrugged. "Probably not, but there is a reason this has come straight to Major Crime. We're dealing with the suspicious death of an infant. Once news gets out, it needs to be seen as being handled as priority."

They left the visitors' car park and headed into the reception area of a large glass-fronted office building. The name of the company 'Carson Bros' was spelt out in large silver font across the reception desk that took up most of the ground space. An overweight woman in her thirties with immaculate make-up looked at them from behind her computer with mild curiosity. The younger woman could have passed as a manager, with her tidy figure dressed in cream silk blouse, pencil knee-length skirt and killer heels, but the man standing behind her looked as if he had just got out of bed. It was obvious at first glance that he was not a visiting businessman; an almost transparently thin white shirt, accessorised with a maroon red tie and black trousers, that needed a once-over with a hot iron. The receptionist directed her attention to the young woman as she enquired how she could help.

Hammond answered by showing his identification card and explained his visit with as little information as he could give. He had noted the receptionist's snobby dismissal of him, and it irritated him. Dunn smiled politely but remained silent.

David Hargreaves found them seated in leather tub chairs near the window. He shook their hands firmly, but his voice betrayed his anxiety as he sat opposite them.

"Please forgive me seeing you here, but I couldn't afford to allow my colleagues to hear what happened this morning. The walls are so thin." He smiled weakly at them both and offered them coffee, which they both accepted.

Hammond sat forward in the chair. "You feel responsible?"

"Yes, of course I feel responsible! I may have caused the death of a child!" Hargreaves looked away from them suddenly, focusing his attention on the view of the car park outside for several seconds before turning back. "Will I be charged with manslaughter?"

Hammond attempted to appear reassuring. "We need to investigate how the child came to be on the road first. Whoever left the baby is responsible for endangering its life, which is why we need to establish their identity and their reasoning." He opened his hands as he spoke. It was important that he came across as trustworthy and not one to judge too quickly.

David Hargreaves looked perplexed, his eyes darting from Hammond to Dunn for several seconds.

The coffee was not the best but it was a good distraction from Hargreaves' anxiety. Hammond sipped it slowly before setting the cup to the side. "You mentioned to the attending officers that you saw a white van with its back doors open driving ahead of you? Did you see anything come out of the vehicle?"

There was a responding shake of the head. "No. I couldn't really see that well. I can say for sure that there were no brake lights, nothing to suggest that the van tried to slow down or stop. To be honest, it all happened so quickly."

Hammond quickly changed tack. "Did you see anyone on the side of the road? Any pedestrians?"

"No. None at all. It was practically an empty road. I think I would have noticed anyone walking on the pavement because it would seem so unusual at that time of the morning."

"What is the situation at home? Are you married? Have a partner?"

The man looked taken aback by the sudden change in tone. He paused before answering. "I'm married, have been for several years. Why?"

Hammond didn't reply. He was watching Hargreaves closely, hoping for a reaction – however small – that would feed his curiosity. Dunn shifted uncomfortably in her seat, willing Hammond to answer, but the silence continued. She arranged what she hoped was a neutral expression.

"In circumstances such as these," she commented, "it is good to have people around you."

"Work distracts me," Hargreaves replied.

Hammond wasn't satisfied with his answer. "Do you know anyone who was pregnant or due to give birth at this time? A girlfriend, for example?"

Hargreaves looked bewildered by the question. He looked at Dunn expectantly, wanting her to clarify. Instead, she waited for his answer.

"Oh, I get it. You think that I was responsible for chucking a baby out of my car? Is that it?" Hargreaves' voice got louder. "The idea is sick! How could you even think such a thing?"

The outburst had attracted attention, and Hammond was aware of the receptionist watching them. The nosy cow needed to mind her own business. He sat forward in his chair so that his knees were almost touching Hargreaves'.

"David, you must understand that it is my duty to consider all possibilities. My opinion of what you may or may not be capable of is not relevant. What is relevant is that we have an unclaimed newly-born infant abandoned in a dangerous environment. We do not know who the mother is. The child may have been snatched from her as she gave birth; there could be a woman in desperate need of medical attention that may not even be aware that her child was left to die. Until we get the results of a post-mortem examination, we cannot even say for sure that you are responsible for the child's death. However, you are our only witness, which means you are currently our only source of information. What you know, may have seen, or even what you believe to be relevant, is vital to us. Do you see?" Hammond held Hargreaves' gaze for a prolonged moment, taking a sip of coffee as he waited for the other man to digest the significance of his words.

"A child has died. We need to know how." He tried a different tactic. "We owe it to the child, if no-one else."

The latter comment worked. Hargreaves looked at Hammond before nodding. "I'll give you any information you need."

*

The heat in the car was stifling, and Hammond opened all the windows before leaving the car park. He could feel the eyes of the receptionist watching every move he and Dunn had made since exiting the building. Maybe she would have been more accepting if he had shaved that morning.

"So much for letting him do all the talking!" Dunn smiled as she spoke, but Hammond knew she was irritated.

He hadn't involved her in the interview but she had been an asset nonetheless. Her feminine charms could have been enough to have distracted a guilty man's persona to slip even a little, but the fact that Hargreaves' vulnerability hadn't been hidden through pride or bravado meant it was more likely the man's remorse was genuine.

"We got what we wanted. At least for now. However, it is worth doing a background check, just to make sure."

Dunn nodded. "It seems a bit odd to go to work after such an experience, though. Being involved in a traffic accident is a good enough reason to miss a day off work for some, especially if there is a fatality."

"You think that is reason to be suspicious?"

Dunn was quiet for several minutes, her gaze focused on the passing landscape before she turned her head to answer Hammond directly.

"I'm always suspicious. It makes me good at my job."

CHAPTER TWO

Wallace Hammond leaned forward on the desk so that he was directly facing Acting Superintendent Brian Morris. His report was brief.

"So far, all we have to work on is an unmarked white van travelling towards Ashford in the early hours of the morning. It shouldn't be too difficult to trace, providing it doesn't have false plates. There is no CCTV along the stretch of road where the infant was hit, but there are speed cameras about a mile ahead which would have recorded it if it was speeding, as Hargreaves claimed. There is no tyre residue to indicate heavy braking, nothing on the verge to suggest that the baby was left at the side of the road. Our only witness is Hargreaves himself. There is not much to suspect him of. He has no record, and so far his story checks out."

"What about the preliminary examination of the infant?"

Morris leaned back further in the office chair. The gap between the wall and the back of the chair was limited, but his new position enabled his long legs to bend and fit under the desk. He looked uncomfortable yet still radiated an air of authority.

Dunn passed the photographs taken from the scene. "The umbilical cord was still attached to the body. It looks like it has been severed using a blunt knife of some kind, possibly a pen-knife," she said. "The medical examiner estimated that the baby had been born very recently, with the reasoning that there was evidence of partial anoxia; the lower limbs were still rather blue. Further investigation could indicate cyanosis, but the medical examiner thought it was more likely to be immature blood circulation. The chest had expanded, which indicated the infant had taken in air before it died. However, all this suggests is that the baby was not stillborn."

Morris interrupted by sighing loudly. Hammond noted the man had aged quickly during the three years since they had begun working together. Initially, Hammond had resented his good looks and his arrogance. Morris was a high achiever who had climbed the ranks steadily through accelerated promotion and management schemes. He was ambitious and egotistical; traits that Hammond found distasteful. Yet over the years he had come to relate to the man whose seemingly idyllic life had been no more perfect than the pictures he had once used to decorate his office. The images of his smiling children and attractive wife had long been stored in the bottom drawer. Now Morris had achieved the typical successful detective status: divorced and work-burdened.

Morris clasped his hands together and addressed them both.

"Ok. We have a problem. Firstly, Dunn, do not even bother skimming over the medical notes yet, because I am unconvinced they are useful at this stage. Only a thorough post-mortem will help us to determine whether the baby was in fact alive or otherwise when it was hit by Hargreaves' car. No amount of blustering about cyanosis or anoxia will convince me that you know what you are talking about. Leave the medical reports to the experts. Your job..." He pointed at Hammond and Dunn with two fingers, ignoring Dunn's reddening face "...is to establish whether there were any witnesses to the baby's birth. Did anyone hear a baby crying? Any evidence....." Morris emphasised the latter word "...that proves the baby was alive before it was hit by the car, other than medical hypothesis."

Hammond, aware of Dunn's humiliation, took over. "Sir, I think what Dunn was trying to highlight was that, on initial superficial evaluation, there was no sign that the baby had lived for very long. As you can see, the infant's head was elongated and the body had a covering of vernix. From the initial images, it is difficult to see a cause of death. We know that Hargreaves collided with the infant, but there was no residue on his car tyres, only a trace on the passenger side bumper, which suggests the infant had been hit from the side or been propelled – such as being forcibly ejected from a moving vehicle. We've ruled out that the baby was thrown from Hargreaves' car because there is no obvious sign that the infant had been in the car with him. Neither did it appear that Hargreaves had a passenger, although this would be difficult to prove since we only have his word that he did not pick anyone up during his journey to work and there are no witnesses."

Morris held up a hand to stop Hammond's rambling. "Like I said, we have a problem. It is important that we investigate this as thoroughly as we can. But until we can identify the mother and the person responsible for the baby being on a road, we are at a dead end. I can't afford to stretch our budget any further than I need to. We have other cases that need the manpower and the technical analysis that I cannot apply to this case. We need more information before we can justify whether this is a criminal investigation or a terrible accident."

Dunn uttered a deliberate cough voicing her disapproval, but Morris chose to ignore her.

"Get the post-mortem out of the way. Appeal for witnesses; send a personal message to the birth mother via the media. Do your best to be diplomatic, and for God's sake, Hammond, look smart. Your priority is to find the mother, then track down the driver of the van and compare their story. If necessary, get forensics to do an examination of the vehicle's interior. I hope you find something, because until you do, you're on your own with this one."

He opened his hands as a half-hearted apology before closing the preliminary report file and sliding it back across the desk to Dunn. "Keep me updated."

*

SHOES ON A WIRE

Hammond opened his apartment door with a determined resolve not to look down. He goose-stepped over the doormat that bid him a faded welcome, and set his first foot homeward straight onto the hallway carpet. It was an action he had repeated for the last three days, and although he had chosen the doormat purposely to prevent the first step indoors contaminating the carpet, the envelope that had lain there since it had invaded his rented home at the beginning of the week had discouraged any interest in the area where the mail had fallen. The door was pushed closed with a raised foot.

Without bothering to bend down, he shook himself free of his shoes, muttering words of rejection as the heel of his sock stubbornly clung to the heel tab of his left leather shoe before pushing the footwear against the wall. Hammond then proceeded along the short corridor to the small living room. With a disgruntled sigh, he surveyed the room before him noting the heap of clean washing he had collected from the launderette at least a week ago and had piled onto the armchair for sorting.

The glass tumbler with the residue of silky brown cognac was where he had left it the previous night, on the carpet beside the pile of reading books he had meant to return to the library before Easter. The furniture was basic: an armchair with brownish grey upholstery, worn bare on the arms and headrest; a small mahogany veneered coffee table, which provided a perch for the oversized television. All had been purchased second-hand. The intention had been to replace furniture he had lost in a house fire three years previously with specially selected antique furniture but, like most intentions, he had never found the time.

He was tired and disgruntled, mainly from his conversation with Morris; the man was infuriatingly obnoxious. But also because the envelope on the doormat taunted him whenever he was alone in the apartment. He walked around the chair, and past the empty bookshelf to the kitchenette. Here, he relaxed. His shoulders sank with relief as he shuffled his way in his worn socks to the fridge, retrieved a ready-meal from the middle shelf, removed the cardboard sleeve, and pricked the film with a fork several times before placing the container in the microwave. He pressed the minute button six times and waited for the ping.

The kitchen chair was pulled away from the circular pine table and he plonked himself down to eat. Despite his hunger and the long-awaited anticipation of a hot meal, Hammond ate the food without enthusiasm. The carton label told him he was eating Beef Stroganoff, but he could not distinguish the taste as being anything recognizable. The food wasn't bland; it was just that Hammond's attitude towards food was one of complacency. He needed to eat, but food did not tempt him in the way it used to; it was no longer a pleasure.

During the last year, he had lost so much weight that he was wearing clothes he wouldn't have been able to get into ten years ago. At 55 years of age, he was in better shape than he had ever been, but it had been unintentional. The reason was staring back at him from the empty chairs around the table, and he knew what was to blame. He was lonely. The truth of the matter embarrassed him. He was a grown man, perfectly capable of looking after himself. His days were filled with work commitments; he had no time for a relationship.

Also, past experience had taught him that women were not to be trusted. The last time he had been tempted, he had paid dearly. He had lost his home, nearly his own life, the life of a dear friend, and then of course, the life of a colleague. Detective Constable Michael Galvin had died three years ago, on the brink of becoming a new father. He had supported Hammond's lonely crusade to investigate a series of dubious suicides at the request of his former commanding officer Lloyd Harris. Driven by loyalty and pig-headedness, Hammond had opened a Pandora's Box. He had exposed a criminal organization involving Harris's ex-girlfriend and daughter – the beautiful Kathleen, who had wasted no time in seducing Hammond for her own needs. And while he had fallen for it, Galvin had paid the ultimate price.

The stroganoff was now cold. Hammond poked at it with the fork but the congealed mess was less appetizing than ever. He got up from the chair, threw the food into the bin and rummaged through the grocery cupboard until he found a cereal bar. Then he retreated to the armchair in the other room where the cognac was waiting for him. The cereal bar was inserted between his lips whilst he used both hands to unscrew the cognac bottle, when the phone rang.

Hammond checked the screen for caller ID and saw with relief that it wasn't work calling him back.

"It's me," the voice was toned with familiarity.

"Paul, how are you?" The bottle was placed on the floor.

"Good. You?" The tone of his son's voice was hesitant, yet apparently not interested enough in his father's welfare to wait for a reply before he proceeded with the reason for his call. "I wondered if you had heard from Mum yet."

The envelope. "You mean, have I received the invitation?"

"Oh, so you did get it. Mum was wondering why you hadn't replied."

Hammond's answer was ready. Because I have no desire to see another man marry my own wife, because I cannot bear to see his smug face and be told how much he loves her, how he will make a better husband than I did. How I failed my own son by making her so miserable she walked out on me and left me with a broken heart.

But instead, Hammond lied. "Only just got it, I was about to call her."

"So, you're coming?"

The cereal bar became the focus of visual interest as Hammond searched his brain for the right words to say. "I'm busy, really snowed under, Paul. The work is stacked up at the moment. I am sure your mum will understand."

"You're joking, right?" Again, there was no opportunity to answer the rhetorical question. "You could at least show some support! You haven't even met Cameron yet. Surely you could make an effort to be civil?"

"Paul, I'm sorry, can't this wait? I am really tired, just got in..." Hammond's voice tailed off.

The silence at the other end told him Paul had disconnected the call.

CHAPTER THREE

A few minutes before eight the following morning, Hammond was seated in the briefing room reading the background information Dunn had gathered on David Hargreaves. It wasn't enlightening. Hargreaves had been married for the last 15 years, and been employed with Carson Bros. for 12 years, starting as an admin clerk before gradually clawing his way to the role of Managing Director for Business Development, earning 45k per annum. He wasn't in debt, other than owing a hefty mortgage and private schooling bills for his two teenage daughters. There had been no previous convictions; not even an unpaid parking ticket. In short, David Hargreaves was a regular guy who had been in the wrong place at the wrong time.

The report on Hargreaves' car held no surprises either. It was roadworthy and clean; nothing to indicate Hargreaves had harboured a newborn baby in the vehicle. The serious collision team had written a basic report by compiling evidence from the road surface, and confirmed that Hargreaves had driven within the speed limit. The nearest hospital had been unable to offer any helpful information; they were unaware of a patient leaving the hospital intra-partum or having admitted a woman who had shown signs of just giving birth, other than the registered patients on the labor ward.

Hammond sighed heavily; the elusive tip-off wasn't going to materialise. He was facing a dead-end. He re-examined the photographs of the infant and traced the outline of the child's features with his forefinger. For a brief moment, he went back in time. The memories of his son as a newborn were vivid and colourful, despite being 26 years earlier, He remembered the perfectly shaped fingernails, the curl of hair, and the downy skin. He recalled the intense pride he had felt cradling his son for the first time.

This infant had died alone, though. Hammond wondered whether the child's birth had even been wanted, or whether it had been feared. He did not want to judge; the complexities of the human condition never ceased to mystify him. He understood all too well that the chemicals caused by hormonal fluctuations during childbirth could cause a temporary psychosis, yet the death of an infant always seemed to bring out the most intense reaction in the public. The mother, if she were ever discovered, would be publicly judged without empathy.

Lost in his deliberations, he was unaware of Dunn's entrance into the room until she seated herself on the chair beside him.

"Sorry, I couldn't find any biscuits, but I got you a coffee."

A brightly coloured mug with a chipped handle was placed in front of him, followed by pages of printed notes wanting his attention. Hammond skimmed the contents; a photocopied invoice threatened to dishearten him even more.

"The white van seen by Hargreaves was picked up by a speed camera passing near the main roundabout, and traced to a vehicle hire firm. The Vauxhall Combo 1700 Twinport had been hired to a man with an Eastern European accent whose driving licence turned out to be forged. We have got the photo from the copied ID, but there are no definitive matches of his features on the database. He could have used the usual disguise tactics and changed his hair, or whatever. All we have is a basic description: slim build; older than middle-aged; and smelt like a heavy smoker. According to the manager, the van was meant to be returned before nine yesterday morning, but it failed to show up. They have been told to contact us if it is returned, but I'm not holding my breath."

Hammond nodded, his attention focused on the images of the dead baby. Following his gaze, Dunn leaned over to take a closer look at the photographs.

"It looks like it is sleeping."

"Yes, *he* does." Hammond did not know why he had reacted so defensively, but as soon as the words left him, he realised he was acting less objectively than he would like.

Dunn's eyebrows rose slightly but she chose to ignore the correction. "So, what are your thoughts?"

Hammond shrugged, then leaned back in his chair and sipped the coffee. It was too sweet, but he was grateful for the moisture. "It could just be a case of child neglect with a nasty ending. A rash decision, or a moment of panic..." His voice trailed off as he took another sip.

Dunn was watching him closely. "But your instinct is telling you it's more than that."

"That's true. However, you know the game. Instinct means sod all if there is no supporting evidence."

Dunn returned the images to the table, mimicking Hammond's pose by leaning back further in her chair. "The post-mortem report isn't in yet, but the baby's features give us a clue. See the nostrils? They are diamond-shaped. The eyes are darker, not blue like most newborn Caucasian babies. That could suggest an Eastern European ancestry."

Unlike Morris, Dunn did not rely purely on facts to aid their investigations; she was a creative thinker who applied her imagination when lack of evidence made facts elusive. Hammond's appreciation of her theories, however, was wasted in this instance.

"I'm not sure that anthropology is going to help us much, Dunn. Human features are simply a response to their environment; there is so much integration now within any one environment that differences between races are minute. However, I see what you are getting at. We may be dealing with a foreigner who wants to stay under the radar from social services."

"That would explain why the infant was abandoned away from any buildings or the chance of being seen. But why leave the baby at the side of the road? Why not leave it at the hospital, or a church?"

"For the same reason a baby was dumped in a stream in Lancashire, and another left at a recycling plant in Scunthorpe within the last 18 months. It is happening everywhere in Britain, hence the ongoing petitions for safe-haven laws in the UK. Unlike the USA, we cannot grant criminal immunity to a parent who abandons their child, hence the fear of being caught."

"It still doesn't make sense to me." Dunn swallowed her drink with exaggerated gulps. "What if Hargreaves witnessed something without realizing the significance? What if the infant was thrown from the back of a van?"

"Then we are dealing with something else entirely. The fact that the child was thrown from a moving vehicle suggests that there are people, rather than one individual person, responsible for the infant's death. It shows conscious thought; an act of malicious intent. What's more, it shows that the child may have been taken from the birth mother forcibly and cruelly."

"What exactly does your instinct tell you?"

Hammond sighed heavily, combing his hands through his hair as if trying to lighten the weight of his loaded paranoid thoughts.

"It tells me we could be looking at an abduction."

*

The post-mortem report was, as Hammond expected, non-conclusive. Without any antepartum, intrapartum, or postpartum medical records, it was not possible to determine whether the infant had been capable of achieving a separate existence once it had been expelled from its mother. Upon superficial examination, the body showed severe bruising, but the markings could not be distinguished as being introduced before or after death, or whether they were indicative of injuries, pre-existing disease, or markings associated with treatment following the birth, such as attempted resuscitation. The umbilical cord, still attached to the body, lacked the reddening of the skin usually seen in an infant from 36 hours after birth. This helped to establish that the baby had been newly-born but gave no evidence whether the manner of birth had attributed to its death or that the infant had survived following expulsion from the birth canal.

Upon internal examination, extraneous material was discovered in the air passages. The lungs were examined closely. The dark purple colouring of the internal tissue indicated an immature respiratory mechanism; the diaphragm had risen, although it was noted that this could have been caused by resuscitation attempts by the paramedics. It was not evidence that the infant had breathed independently after complete extrusion from the mother's birth canal.

The absence of material in the digestive tract confirmed the infant had not been nursed following birth. The infant's brain had been inspected. Subdural haemorrhage was evident, but the pathologist would not state whether the bleeding around the brain had occurred as a result of maternal vitamin K deficiency, physical trauma during the birth, or as a result of being clipped by Hargreaves' car. Similarly, the retinal haemorrhage and damage to the chest wall was noted to have been caused either during attempted resuscitation or even indicative of post-mortem phenomena.

The deficiency of oxygen in the blood was hypothesised to be the underlying factor attributing to the death of the newborn, but no one cause was evident other than the interruption of respiration following difficulties during birth or treatment post-partum.

In short, the cause of death was attributed to "mechanical asphyxia".

Hammond groaned inwardly. He was familiar with the term and knew that numerous natural and unnatural causes could be covered within the one diagnosis. The results would not help to support a criminal investigation. Instead, it meant that the whole process of investigation would be delayed whilst a second, maybe even a third forensic pathologist's opinion could be sought. Skimming further down the report, he looked for clues for something that could help identify the baby's mother. Residual blood and body fluids found on the skin and in the cavities of the infant had been sent for analysis. All Hammond could hope for was that the DNA would match a profile in their system.

The appeal for public information was scheduled to take place in the afternoon, and there remained some hope that the mother would be found. The thirst for closure, for an explanation, could be overpowering at times, but it was counter-balanced by the expectation to be disappointed.

Hammond stood up from the table and stretched his back, walking over to the window. For several minutes he stood in quiet contemplation, watching the activity of cars and pedestrians outside. Sometimes it felt as if he were detached from the normal life seen in the daily bustle. There lacked a routine to this work; there was no beginning or end to any one day. No day was the same. It used to be the one factor that he had enjoyed about his job – the thrill, the lack of monotony. But as he had aged, Hammond had begun to see it differently.

Even when a case was solved, the perpetrators apprehended and charged, the personal reactions and the deliberations that had been consistent throughout the investigations remained and lingered. Wherever he went, he would associate a place to an investigation he had worked on earlier. When a case was filed as unsolved, the frustration never left, the desire to find answers stayed as constant as criminal activity. Hammond sighed, digging his hands deeper in his pockets. It was beginning to get dark. A grey cloud was heading towards Folkestone; storms had been predicted.

He turned back to the papers on the table. They could wait before he shared them with Morris. He needed to get out of the office. He waited until he had reached the privacy of his car before he dialled Paul's number.

*

The appeal was aired on television by three in the afternoon. It had been decided that no photographs would be released to the media, although the local news channel had used a random image of a baby wrapped in a blanket to highlight the plight of an abandoned child. Hammond had chosen his words carefully; he did not give details of the suspected manner of death, but instead focused on the importance of tracing the mother. Her welfare was a concern, he had emphasised.

Hammond watched the playback with Morris during the news programme.

"There is not much else we can do at the moment." Without the van, there could be no forensic examination of the rental vehicle, so no other evidence could substantiate Hargreaves' account; Morris was unwilling to spend any more resources on the investigation. "We just have to hope that someone comes forward as a result of the appeal. Until then, I am not confident we have much of a case to work on."

Hammond kept silent. He had wanted a better outcome but knew that his instinct was not enough to justify a continued investigation. He had to follow clues, and there were no more clues to follow, it was as simple as that. All possibilities had been exhausted: missing people had been reviewed; hospitals, hotels, and public services were on alert. Whatever Hammond suspected, he could not establish in fact. He acknowledged Morris's decision with a nod. Outside, it had started to rain.

Paul wasn't answering his phone. Hammond ended up leaving messages for him in half a dozen places before finally relenting and calling Jenny – Paul's best friend, the daughter Hammond had never had. Or as Jenny had put it, the daughter he never used to have but did now.

She wasn't surprised to hear from him.

"I heard you had shared words," she said.

"Actually, we didn't. I want to speak but he is avoiding me."

There was a sound of sucking on the other end. Hammond didn't need to see the e-cigarette that seemed to be permanently attached to her lower lip since her attempts to stop smoking had failed.

"You can't blame him, Wally. He's pissed."

"Because I won't go to his mum's wedding? Come on! She doesn't really want me there anyway!"

"But Paul does. He was hoping you would meet the lady in his life."

Lightning streaked the heavens above, and for a moment Hammond was fixated on watching the blue flashes drawing closer. He rolled the car window down. The atmosphere was rich; the smell of the rain sweet and earthy.

"He has a girlfriend? Is it serious?"

"Oh yeah... Trust me, Wally, you will want to meet this one." Jenny laughed "Look, give him a few days to cool off. You know how over-sensitive he can be. Don't worry, you'll hear from him soon." She blew a kiss down the phone before ending the call.

Hammond sat in the car for a long time, digesting Jenny's news. His relationship with Paul had always been tumultuous. The boy was very loyal to his mother, always had been, even though it had not been necessary to choose sides. Hammond wished his ex-wife the best; he had just wanted the best to be himself rather than the new groom.

For an inexplicable moment, he felt the need to weep. He quickly turned the ignition and selected first gear. As he left the car park, Hammond made a mental note to remind Jenny he did not like being called Wally.

CHAPTER FOUR

Hammond had slept badly. He had lain awake for several hours listening to the couple from the basement apartment arguing. The words were indecipherable, but the alternating pitches of sounds were easy to interpret; the highs of hysteria and the lows of angry muttering were familiar and unwelcome. Finally, in the early hours, after the last door had slammed, there was peace. But it was an unsettled silence; like the calm before a storm.

Hammond kept expecting the arguing to suddenly resume. Occasionally he drifted into a confused state, where he dreamt he was awake but wanting to sleep. Then he would awake feeling exhausted and frustrated. Hammond hated the apartment. He hated the neighbours being in such close proximity, but he wasn't ready to go house hunting. The house that he had loved had been a family home in Stanford. The home where his wife had baked in the kitchen, where Hammond had stored his prized LPs and books, where his son had played in the garden. It had been in a permanent state of chaos, messy and in need of decorating, but it had been Hammond's sanctuary – even when Lyn had walked out of the house and the marriage with packed bags and an angry hand gesture, when Paul had left for university and not returned. Even when the house had burned to ruins, almost taking Hammond with it. It had always been a home.

By the time Hammond had divided the remaining assets with Lyn, it would have been possible to have used what was left of the insurance money on a cheaper house, maybe not in a prime location, but something on the town outskirts. Somewhere like Hythe, with a small garden that wasn't over-looked or possibly a balcony with sea views, where Hammond could read his books and drink his cognac in peace. But there seemed no point. It wouldn't be a home without being able to share it with the people he loved. So instead, he had resigned himself to working as much as he could, finding ways to occupy his days and his thoughts, returning to the apartment with its hateful furniture and dismal surroundings only to sleep.

By five o'clock all hope of resting was abandoned. Hammond got up, padded his way into the bathroom and relieved himself into the toilet, noting his urine was dark amber. The dry metallic taste in his mouth was gargled away with mouthwash. His jaw ached. The tension ran from the back of his ear to the side of his neck. He massaged the area and debated whether to have a bath, decided he couldn't be bothered, and got under the shower instead. The water was tepid warm, but it was good enough.

He dressed in the toweling robe hanging from the bathroom door and ventured into the living room to sort the clothes piled on the armchair. Finding the blue striped shirt he thought he had lost months ago, he went in search of the iron, locating it under the kitchen sink; the cord wrapped tightly round the handle. He filled the reservoir using water from the kitchen tap, then searched for an ironing board, remembered he didn't have one, and laid the shirt onto the kitchen table instead. The iron spluttered and water cascaded over the shirt, but he was satisfied at the first sign of steam. The shirt became the object of early morning, sleep-deprived focus, all creases smoothed. By the time the iron was switched off, the shirt hung on the back of the kitchen door, Hammond's mind felt a good deal clearer.

He had filled the kettle, laid strips of bacon under the grill and was in the process of slicing the bread, when his phone rang. He checked the clock; it was ten minutes to seven.

Normally, he would be groaning at the inconvenient time at which he was summoned to a scene of a suspected crime, but on this occasion, he felt relief at the impending distraction.

"Hammond."

"Did I wake you?" The voice at the other end was instantly recognizable – DS Tom Edwards, Hammond's trusted colleague within the Major Crime Department.

"Actually, no, but would it make a difference in this case?"

"The coastguard just got a call from Marine Life Rescue. They were in the process of rescuing a stranded porpoise near Shakespeare Cliff, when they spotted what seemed to be a group of people lying unresponsive on the beach at the Langdon Bay."

Hammond thought rapidly. Langdon cliffs stretched just over two miles towards South Foreland Lighthouse. There were numerous paths crisscrossing the coast walk. It was possible someone had fallen off the cliff edge, but the report stated people rather than one person. One falling off a cliff was likely; a group of people falling together seemed less so. A suicide pact?

"Do you know how many people? Are they confirmed fatalities?"

"The report is still coming in, from what I have gathered so far. Medics have been called but I got the impression there is at least one fatality."

"Who do you have on call at the moment?"

"Dunn is on her way, and I'm heading out to Dover now. Morris has instructed you to be the SIO until we know what we are dealing with."

"Fine. I'll meet you there."

Hammond turned off the grill. The smell of the cooking bacon was almost too irresistible to ignore, but he promised himself to make up for it later. He glanced out of the kitchen window overlooking London Street, trying to determine what kind of weather they were dealing with. The storm had passed but the August humidity was promising to stay a while longer.

A hot and sticky atmosphere wasn't the most hospitable when dealing with corpses. He threw on his shirt and continued to dress hurriedly whilst he hunted for his car keys. The apartment door slammed shut after him with great effect; the final crescendo concluding the Night of the Sleepless Suite.

*

The chalk underfoot was still slippy from the previous day's downpour. Hammond walked for several minutes along the cliff top until he reached the narrow footpath that zigzagged down the cliff-face. Wishing he was wearing shoes with a better grip than his leather lace-ups, he stepped carefully, leaning heavily onto the handrail to steady himself. It was not a gracious approach and he hoped his colleagues below were not witnessing his arrival.

Eventually the path sloped onto a wooden gangplank leading to the abandoned shelters that had once housed the coastal searchlights. Police cordon tape had been tied across the rusted iron doors, blocking off the entrance into the tunnels that had once served as bunkers in the Second World War but were now a popular hideout for delinquents. He showed his ID to one of the officers and was directed towards a metal ladder fixed to the chalk face, leading to the beach eight metres below.

There were several people on the beach. Some were occupied with taking photographs of the scene, or processing any possible evidence that hadn't been washed away by the incoming tide; most were clustered near large chalk boulders sheltered under the overhanging cliff. Hammond scanned the scene before him as his feet rolled clumsily over the large pebbles.

DS Lois Dunn was talking to a man dressed in an oilskin jacket that reached down to his mid-calf. *The man was evidently more prepared*, Hammond thought, noting the black rubber boots that enabled him to stand with such poise on the unwelcoming terrain. Hammond didn't recognise him but was instantly aware that the man was not the kind you would forget easily. Tall and broad-shouldered, he stood with his legs slightly apart in a steadying yet confident manner. His chin was square, his long nose perfectly aligned between chiseled cheekbones. His head was bowed, and it was evident his eyes were intently focused on Dunn's mouth as she spoke.

Hammond couldn't hear what Dunn was saying, but her body language spoke volumes. One leg was stuck out at an awkward angle, causing her weight to rest on one hip, and her hands hung limply by her sides. She looked self-conscious; her usual facade of confidence absent. The woman was turning to jelly.

Hammond strode over with an outstretched hand, expecting Dunn to snap into action and introduce him. But instead she stood, mouth slightly agape as if she had forgotten the purpose of her being there. Before Hammond could utter a word, he was scrutinised by a pair of the bluest eyes he had ever seen.

"Who are you?"

The voice was too loud. It demanded attention and expected subservience, and Hammond took only seconds to know he didn't like this man.

Slightly taken aback, he drew himself to his full height, trying to ignore the fact that his feet were getting wet. "My name is DI Wallace Hammond. I am the Senior Investigating Officer."

The man smiled a lazy curve of the lips. "No, DI Hammond. This looks likely to be a Category A, so I have been allocated as SIO for today. I was just informing your Sergeant Dunn here that I will be handling this case, although you are very welcome to assist me."

The man had an accent, possibly French, and the words flowed off his tongue like butter on a hot crumpet. He stood before Hammond and proffered his I.D. "I am Detective Chief Inspector Xavier Hunt," he said, before turning to walk away.

He continued to address them over his shoulder as he led them towards the sandy corner of the beach. "These unfortunate people were moved earlier by the coastguards and brought closer to the cliff edge. They are all deceased and were so when the coastguard arrived at the scene. The tide was coming in when we got here. As you can see, I have directed that a trench be dug in the sand around the boulders to keep away the water and help us process any possible evidence present on the bodies. However, it won't help us for much longer."

Hammond tried to hide his irritation. Tempted though he was to respond with criticism, he kept quiet and concentrated instead on the scene in front of him. The deceased were three males and one female. They looked young. Hammond estimated the eldest was no older than his mid-twenties. Two of the men were dusky-skinned; one was bearded, with jet black curly hair. The third male was Caucasian with pubescent downy hair on his cheeks and chin. The female's face was covered; her long dark hair was strewn across her face, hiding her features.

Their clothing suggested they were not local, and they were dressed inappropriately for the season. The men were wearing tracksuit trousers; one man was barefoot, another in sandals, the youngest in trainers. The woman wore leather lace-up shoes, a jumper and long skirt. All had been arranged so that they lay on their backs, their palms facing skyward.

Hammond cleared his throat. "Any idea of how they died? Were they washed up from a capsized boat?"

It wouldn't be the first time. Only two months earlier, British smugglers had attempted to cross the English Channel from Calais with eight stowaways when one vessel had sunk nine miles off the coast of Dover.

DCI Hunt shook his head slightly. "There were no boats nearby when the coastguard arrived and no reports that any boats were seen here during the night, but of course, it is still possible that these people were brought here covertly by dinghy. However, these people didn't drown. There are wounds from having been beaten and also…" He crouched down next to one of the bodies and moved the head gently to the side. The temporal area of the skull was matted with blood and brain debris.

"Shot?" Dunn's voice rang clear; she had regained her composure and was back into efficient mode.

"Possibly. It looks like it. I will not say for sure." Hunt looked up at her from his crouched position as he spoke. He opened his hands and lifted a shoulder in an almost apologetic shrug. "The medical examiner had to work very quickly. He was most displeased the scene had not been preserved. However, with the rising water and the confusion when the bodies were first discovered…" He left the sentence hanging and stood up to his full height. His gaze traced the sky above the coastline.

"We need to take the bodies to the hospital as quickly as we can. The coastguard helicopter will recover these unfortunate people." It was evident Hunt lacked any more information; presumably he had not been at the scene much before Hammond's arrival.

"Do we have the witness accounts from the people who found the bodies?" Hammond bit back the urge to mimic's Hunt's reference to the "unfortunate people".

Hunt turned his attention towards Hammond ready to answer, but was interrupted by his mobile phone ringing. He promptly turned his back to them and walked away, evidently not wanting them to hear his conversation.

Hammond turned to Dunn. "What have you learnt about our new colleague?"

Dunn didn't hide the enthusiasm in her reply. "He's stationed at Coquelles, working with Cross-Channel Intelligence." She paused, her eyes glittering. "Gorgeous, isn't he?"

Hammond's attention changed to selective hearing mode. Instead, he scanned the scene. "Where is Edwards?"

"He's interviewing the Marine Life Rescue people at the coastguard building." Dunn's voice tailed off as she continued to gaze at the retreating back of DCI Hunt.

"Do you know if any photographs or videos were taken at the scene when the bodies were found?" Hammond registered her negative shake of the head. "Ok, in that case we need as much detail as possible from the first responders as to how the bodies were positioned, and any identification that was found on their clothing. There are no bags here, no indication that they had any possessions with them. One of the victims has no shoes. Check that there were no shoes found in the area that have not been accounted for; whether there was any debris, any drug paraphernalia present near the bodies, anything that can give us an idea of where these people came from, which route they took to get here, or why they were here. In the meantime, I'm going to check on Edwards at the coastguard station. I want to listen to the initial call to the coastguard when the bodies were found."

Hammond jerked his head to where Hunt was still talking on the phone and offered an afterthought. "Dunn, don't get too excited. Not all kissed frogs turn out to be princes." He turned on his sinking heels and headed back towards the ladder.

Chapter Five

"The rumor is, our friend Hunt is gay," DS Edwards winked at Hammond and whispered with his hand cupped over his mouth. "The cocksucker from Coquelles!"

Two hours after the first alarm had been raised, several onlookers had gathered at the cliffs in front of the coastguard station, attracted by the sound of the helicopter and the entourage of police cars, forensic investigation vans, and ambulances that crowded the parking area. They stood expectantly behind the police barricade, straining their necks, hoping to see a glimpse of the activity. From within the coastguard station, Hammond's eyes scanned the audience with the hope that one spectator would reveal more than excitement at the drama they were witnessing. He was well aware that criminals often returned to the scene of a crime; some revealed a sense of pride in their achievements through the hint of a smile or a cocky stance. The need to be recognised, to be accredited with the crime, was sometimes the cause of their own downfall.

"Maybe you should tell Dunn that. She needs something to snap her out of her romantic reverie."

Hammond's stomach rumbled loudly, distracting him from his observation. He was finding it difficult to concentrate on the witness statements he was organizing. The thought of crispy bacon wrapped in a crusty French baguette was all-consuming.

"Nah. Too much fun to watch and say nothing! Anyway, the girl is too focused on work lately. She needs some playtime."

Hammond nodded distractedly. He wondered whether a hot drink would suffice and stuck his head out the door, looking down the hall for a kitchen. "Preferably not when we are investigating a case together."

Hammond had admired Dunn's work ethics for all the years they had worked together. He applauded her thoroughness, her ability to apply logic and speak her mind, even when it was in criticism of his own efforts. However, it hadn't escaped his attention that lately she had been outreaching herself. Her efforts to impress Acting Superintendent Morris recently had been embarrassing for them both. There had been a hint of arrogance in her attitude and Hammond didn't like it.

He decided to change the subject. "How do you think the victims got to the beach?"

Edwards shrugged. "The obvious answer would be to say they were taken by boat and killed on the beach."

Hammond was brooding. "But why is that the most obvious assumption?"

Edwards shot a glance at Hammond. "They looked out of place; they way they were dressed suggested they were foreign, Also, the guy had no shoes. Possibly he removed them to walk across the rocks so he didn't slip on the seaweed."

Hammond nodded. Edward's thoughts were logical, but it was almost too tidy an explanation.

"There are numerous nationalities living in and around Dover. Not to mention holiday camps, hostels, and hotels. The victims' attire could be an inherited style, an old-fashioned manner of dress, or frugal living – purchasing clothes from charity shops, for example. We've automatically assumed that the victims are foreign, or that they recently travelled across the Channel immediately prior to their deaths. It's plausible, but it is ludicrous to assume so early on. It is possible that the victims did not travel as a group. Maybe they all travelled separately and met at the beach. The path on the cliff face is a regular route for tourists. Why are they here? A pagan ritual? A suicide pact, maybe? I don't know, but that's the point. We don't know anything, so why are we being so quick to assume we know more than we do?"

Edwards looked almost offended by Hammond's tone. "I didn't assume anything. I was simply suggesting."

Hammond offered an apologetic smile. "I know, Tom. I don't mean anything personal. However, what I am wondering is how did Hunt get there so quickly? He must have more than a presumption the victims were immigrants. What other reason would he have to take over the investigation? I suspect that he knows a lot more than he is letting on."

Edwards shrugged again. His body language became awkward, as if he were worried he may say the wrong thing. He compromised by addressing the information he had already gathered. "There is a treasure hunt site that is popular online around the world. Geocaching, it's called. Apparently, there is a cache hidden in the tunnel above the bay. Treasure hunters have to decipher a clue, locate the "treasure", and then leave their name with the so-called treasure or replace it with something else of the same value. The game is very popular; apparently there are over six million Geocachers worldwide. I've checked the most recent entry for when the treasure was last found in that location. It was dated two weeks ago."

He referred to the papers he had printed off and shuffled them across the table towards Hammond.

"Otherwise, visitors go to the beach to look at the wreckage of the steamship that is visible at low tide. How they got there is one of two possibilities: by footpath or by boat. Why they went there, we may never know, but what happened when they got there may become evident in the post-mortem which will take place at Canterbury. It is just a case of waiting for the results. We have enough to launch a criminal enquiry. I've submitted the pictures to missing persons, but there have been no people answering our victims' descriptions. And there is no more information gathered from the Marine Life Rescuers. They didn't approach the shore. We have the coastguard's statement, with diagrams that show the original positions of the deceased—"

Edwards was interrupted by the appearance of Dunn hurrying into the corridor from the main entrance. Her face was flushed, her voice agitated.

"They've found another one... on the rocks... she's still alive."

*

As Senior Investigating Officer, DCI Hunt decided to remain at the incident room which had been set up for the next 24 hours at the coastguard station. Since there was no precise idea when the murders had taken place, the public were being encouraged to speak to the officers there if they had any information to offer. Forensic examiners were occupied with processing the footpaths and tunnels, looking for any clues.

Hammond and Edwards followed the ambulance with the surviving woman to the hospital. As he drove, Hammond's mind digested the morning's events. He felt uneasy, but he couldn't pinpoint what it was exactly that made his mind so unsettled. The savage attacks on the victims were senseless but he had experienced the aftermath of numerous murders before. There had been times when he had been affected by what he had seen – sleepless nights or a restless imagination – but this case was hinting at becoming something far more complex than a gangland–style execution. The victims had looked so young, so vulnerable.

The pathetic sight of the young man lying on the beach without shoes was retained in his mind. Hammond had seen the young die before, but this felt different somehow. In a way it was a relief that he would not be responsible for heading the investigation. He knew that the next few days would be occupied with examining any possible clues found at the scene, questioning visitors to the site. Had they seen anything suspicious? Heard anything? The questions Hammond wanted answering were launched in his mind, but he was relying on luck. Until then, all he had to go on was what could be told by the woman found clinging to the rocks. If she survived.

Upon arrival at the hospital, the woman was admitted to the Intensive Care Unit. Just as quickly, it became apparent to Hammond that his presence was not welcome. Despite several attempts to question the woman's condition, he was ignored or asked to wait. Which he did, seated on a plastic chair in the corridor, desperately craving a bacon sandwich but unwilling to move away from his position in case the duty consultant became available.

Edwards occupied his time talking to the nurses or the cleaning staff. Hammond watched his colleague with mild irritation. Edwards had a remarkable knack of blending into any environment with ease, but it seemed as if he was content to wait indefinitely. The man carried an air of joviality; he was calm and unhurried, and well respected as an intelligent detective. And despite his occasional disregard for tact and diplomacy, Edwards was never one to deny his devotion to his wife and three children, meaning he had the unique ability to prioritise his family over work. It was a characteristic that Hammond had lacked, and now regretted. The thought of all the time he had wasted chasing criminals rather than spending it with Paul as he grew up suddenly overwhelmed Hammond with sadness. He swallowed hard, causing his throat to ache.

Fed up with waiting, he discreetly indicated to Edwards that he was going into the treatment room. The other man came over immediately. "The nurses were saying she is unconscious, the doctor doesn't expect her to recover soon."

Carefully, Hammond opened the door and stepped inside. Various machines were beside the bed where the woman lay. A nurse looked up from the blood pressure cuff she was applying to a thin arm hanging stiffly from under the bed sheet. "You shouldn't be in here," she said disapprovingly.

"I am a police officer. I need to know how she is doing."

She tutted with obvious disdain at his intrusion, but was distracted by Edward's entrance into the room.

"You must be Claire," he said with a grin. She nodded. "Your colleagues were just saying you have worked here for 12 years. It can't be easy, but must be rewarding," he ended his sentence with a smile.

Despite her resolve to be firm, the nurse returned his grin, clearly flattered by the personal attention. "I'll get the doctor to speak to you."

Hammond moved closer to the bedside. It was the first time he had seen the unconscious patient and he was shocked by what he saw. On first appearances, she looked of Ethiopian origin, with an aquiline nose, small mouth, and an oval face shape. She would have been attractive had the right side of her face not been a mass of discoloured, engorged flesh. Her eyelids were swollen closed, and the scalp was blistered and bald above the temporal area.

"We have asked for there to be no unauthorised persons allowed in this room."

Hammond turned around to face the doctor directly. He saw a very thin man, looking no older than his mid-twenties. "I am authorised." He held out his ID, which the doctor barely glanced at before approaching the patient. Edwards stood at the end of the bed, making notes.

"She was very dehydrated when she arrived; it took a while before we could get a vein. I do not think she has had anything to eat or drink for a long time. There are severe burns to the side of the head and neck, bruising to her upper back and lower limbs. There are lacerations on her wrists and ankles, which indicate she was restrained. I have advised that she is sedated for the time being."

Edwards spoke up. "Will she survive?"

The doctor shrugged. "I honestly do not know. We still need to check for any internal injuries, and we will arrange for x-rays later today, but..." The doctor shook his head slightly. "She is very poorly; I can only hope she pulls through." He offered the two men an apologetic smile as he ushered them towards the door.

"If there is any change, I will contact you. I presume you will want to station an officer outside the door for security?"

Hammond confirmed his answer with a silent nod.

"In that case..." the Doctor continued, ushering them into the corridor and closing the door firmly behind them. "I must insist that they stay outside the room." He shook the detectives' hands and exited down the corridor. Hammond headed straight for the canteen.

*

At four pm, everyone who had attended the scene of the crime gathered at the incident room. More than 12 police officers were either seated or perched on table edges when Hunt entered. He nodded at the room in greeting and shrugged off his jacket, folding it casually on the back of a chair. He introduced himself again and started to go through the preliminary reports.

As Hammond listened, he was aware of a hint of resentment building within him. It had nothing to do with Hunt taking over as Senior Investigating Officer. Hammond wasn't a Chief Inspector and he had no ambition to climb the ranks. He was accustomed to being succeeded by a higher authority, but it irritated him when he was expected to work with what appeared to be compromised intelligence. The Major Crime Department's response had been within minutes of the coastguard's call to control, yet DCI Hunt had been there in enough time to organise forensic examination of the scene as well as delegate the attending officers, all within 20 minutes of that call. It was odd, and suggested that Hunt had somehow been prepared for the event.

Hunt passed photographs of the victims around the room. "I am confident that we are looking for a perpetrator with a personality type between organised and erratic. Organised, because the victims had no identification, possibly any ID had been taken away from them. Their wrists had been restrained so our killer was organised enough to take bondage material. There were marks on the ankles that suggest they had been bound at some point. The ties on the wrists had been removed by the first responders; I presume to check for vital signs." He sighed deeply and shook his head to signify his discontent. "The preliminary examination suggested that all our victims had been deprived of food and fluids. This has yet to be confirmed by the post-mortem, but it does mean we may be looking at a hostage situation.

"Three of the victims had what appeared to be gunshot wounds – to the side of the head on the female, and the neck on one male. The possibility that our killer acts erratically is suggested by the method of killing the fourth victim, who had been beaten with a blunt instrument to the back of the skull, possibly following failure of a first attempt, since there was evidence of scorched tissue on the neck."

Hunt looked at the forensic team hoping for an update. Their report was brief; no significant clues had yet been discovered. Significant staining had been found on pebbles at the scene, probably blood stains which were consistent with the visible wounds on the victims, but nothing could be confirmed until the residue had been analyzed.

Then it was Hammond's turn to talk about the surviving female found on the rocks. He reiterated the information given by the doctor and passed the photocopied diagram showing the injuries found on the woman. The room was silent for several seconds as the severity of the attack sunk in.

"Her injuries are severe, but there is a chance she will survive, in which case we have a better chance of finding out whether she had escaped an attempted execution on the beach or whether she had regained consciousness after the attack and tried to escape detection by the coastguard. However, her position on the rocks does suggest she came from Langdon Bay. There is no other way she could have got to where she was found."

"Are we concentrating on the theory that the victims are not British born?" Dunn was standing by the window, the light coming from behind her creating a halo of auburn around delicate pale features.

Hunt nodded. He straightened his back and smoothed his tie against his chest.

"Yes." His voice was assured.

"You have no hesitation?" Hammond asked. "Surely we should not make assumptions at this stage."

Mild annoyance flashed across the DCI's features before he answered.

"For the time being, I am content to work on the obvious. Our perpetrator is likely to be local, or at least have a thorough knowledge of the local area. Secondly, they are not an opportunistic offender; this involved forethought and planning. However, there are no indications that a party of people had been shepherded down the steep footpath during the last 24 hours. If they were held at gunpoint with their arms restrained behind them, it is likely there would be scuff marks on the chalk face. The footpath is not an easy smooth path, especially when it is wet. There are holes, steep steps, and the remains of tracks from the old mineral railway, so they would have slipped and stumbled at the very least, and there would be subsequent disturbance in the ground or undergrowth. There would be marks, blood smears on the chalk face. So far, we have found none. Yesterday's rainfall would not have obliterated every trace, therefore, we can only presume that they arrived by boat. And why would a British National arrive on British soil covertly?" He looked at Hammond directly as he answered his own question.

"They wouldn't. Unless…" He paused for effect. "…Unless they were complicit in smuggling illegal immigrants onto English soil."

Dunn was convinced by his argument. "So, you think we are looking at a British perpetrator, possibly a racist attack?"

"Not necessarily. The party may have been attacked by one of their own."

Hunt brought the meeting to a conclusion; each officer was assigned to specific objectives for the next twelve hours, with the plan to meet again early the next morning. As Hammond ventured towards the door, Hunt gestured for his attention.

"Can I offer you a coffee?"

The invitation was undeniable, the intention not so obvious. For a moment Hammond wondered whether the man was flirting with him, but his thirst for a hot drink prompted him to accept. A vending machine was finally located at the end of the south-facing corridor.

Hunt handed the plastic cup over to Hammond. "I fear that this case needs to be handled sensitively," he said with the subtle offering of an explanation.

Hammond accepted the drink and the opportunity to speak frankly. "We've unearthed a lot of questions, not so many answers. Yet I suspect you have more answers than you are prepared to share. I am interested in knowing what you are holding back."

Hunt raised his eyebrows, and Hammond was again struck by how clear the other man's eyes were. He wondered if Hunt was wearing contact lenses.

The senior officer leant back against the wall. His casual manner indicated he was willing to continue the conversation away from the team. "The objectives of the Kent European Liaison Unit include obtaining crime intelligence around Kent ports, as I am sure you are aware." He did not wait for Hammond's confirmation. "For the last seven years, I have been working closely with Europol, SOCA, and other European agencies, on an operation targeting suspected people-smuggling gangs. We had evidence that there is an established criminal network assisting illegal immigrants to reach the UK by smuggling them in vehicles through the Channel ports. The majority of migrants intended to travel from the UK to North America using false documents.

"Last week, 100 officers from Immigration Enforcement and our colleagues within Kent Police carried out simultaneous raids on addresses in Kent, Essex, and Surrey. At the same time, several people who had been under observation were arrested in France, Belgium, and Germany. The simultaneous raids benefitted us with the opportunity to seize computers, documents, and mobile phones, all of which held invaluable information on future planned smuggling operations and major players in the criminal community. However..." Hunt paused whilst he took a long sip of his drink.

"...it was impossible to capture every individual responsible. The arrests and the seized intelligence have caused panic amongst those desperate to get into the country undetected. The stakes have gone up, which means there is a greater opportunity for the less sophisticated of smuggling communities to reap in the profits. We have been particularly interested in several individuals owning small sea-faring craft, all of whom have made regular visits to the Kent shoreline," he went on. "They are under the impression that their movements have not been detected, but I have made it my business to monitor them closely. One individual in particular was spotted one mile off the coast, near Sangatte, over 24 hours ago. He had several passengers in the boat with him when he left. On previous occasions, he had returned within 12 hours. However, shortly after midnight, his body was recovered by a French naval helicopter and taken to Boulogne-sur-Mer. It was evident he had been killed and dumped overboard. His boat, though, had been commandeered and continued its journey to Dover."

Hammond understood the man was taking particular care choosing his words. "And you believe that the passengers seen leaving Sangatte were the individuals found at Langdon Bay this morning?"

Hunt nodded. He sipped his coffee slowly. It was obvious he preferred to be prompted with questions rather than to have to give too much information willingly.

"May I ask how you acquired this last bit of intelligence? Is it reliable?"

"Absolutely. The evidence that was seized last week has justified reason to continue our investigation, but it is not enough to shut the whole criminal smuggling network down. For several months we have been using unmanned aircraft to patrol the coastline and the English Channel. The evidence is irrefutable and is yielding results."

There was a pause whilst the two men finished their drinks in silence until Hunt pushed himself away from the wall. He offered Hammond a hint of a smile. "I heard a lot about you prior to meeting you this morning. 'Hammond is like a dog with a bone', they warned me. He won't stop digging until every scrap has been found."

Hammond finished the dregs of his coffee before throwing the empty cup into the wastebin. He replied with equal honesty. "I heard you were gay."

CHAPTER SIX

When the 19-year-old Wallace Hammond had applied to be recruited into the police force in 1977, he had been driven by the desire to be a hero. Not a hero in the eye of his peers, but in the eyes of his father. Senior Hammond had been in awe of law enforcers, and one in particular – Scotland Yard Detective Robert Fabian, the inspiration behind a television series aired in the 1950s. Whilst his friends played football or shared quality time fixing cars with their fathers, the young Wallace Hammond had enjoyed being seated at the dinner table listening to his dad recounting how crimes had been solved using the expertise of psychiatrists, pathologists, and graphologists from decades past. The older man's enthusiasm for the subject had never wavered.

When Hammond was recruited into the Kent Constabulary as a constable, his father had already died of a heart attack, but there had remained the hope that his father had been aware of his son's achievement. As Hammond gained experience, his objectives changed. He appreciated working on the frontline of human emotions, witnessing people when they were at their worst and their most vulnerable.

Contrary to his childish ideal, Hammond did not become a hero. No-one had shown appreciation for him turning up in his MK2 Ford Granada at all hours with a flashing blue light and an objective to help someone in need. Instead, he was seen as a nuisance, a killjoy. But it didn't matter. By then, Hammond had grown to love the thought that he wasn't doing a job; he was fulfilling his life's purpose. He was constantly being tested as to who he was, the choices he made, the sacrifices he was willing to commit. In his 36-year long career, Hammond had seen eight colleagues die whilst on duty. He had witnessed the most extreme of human conditions; met the most compassionate and the most feared. He had unraveled numerous murders, rapes, burglaries, and kidnappings. He had returned people to their loved ones, given closure to the grieving, helped people make better choices with their lives. But as a result, he had lost his own sense of direction. The future, as Hammond now saw it, was one that would be spent alone. The hero that Hammond had once aspired to be would have had the admiration and the love of the people he protected. The police officer that Hammond had become had no more than a failed marriage behind him, a son who did not understand him, and a home he hated coming back to.

Hammond's reverie was all consuming. From the moment he had sunk down into the armchair, his thoughts had become restless and disorientating. He had left his colleagues with the strongest temptation to tell them he wouldn't be returning to work in the morning, nor any day after. But he had kept silent, simply nodded, and got into his car with the schedule agreed for the next day. The feeling of dissatisfaction with his work was natural; no matter how one was driven by a sense of purpose, there would be the inevitable doubt that they were doing enough with their lives. But this was different.

It was not the first time Hammond had considered retiring. The last two years in particular had been unsettling enough to challenge any officer's dedication to the force. The coalition government had cut funding to Kent Police by 20 percent, which had resulted in thousands of police personnel being made redundant and 200 newly recruited constables were unable to fulfill their employment. In 2011, the London riots had weakened the morale of law enforcers throughout the city and the neighbouring counties. And the threat of continued disorder was recognised by every officer, citing worsening social and economic conditions as a potential cause. 2012 had promised regenerated confidence with events such as the Queen's Diamond Jubilee and the London Olympics, both requiring resources from the neighbouring forces, yet out of the £500million budget spent on security, Kent Police didn't receive a penny. The fate of the force was to be left in the hands of the newly elected Police and Crime Commissioner. Hammond scoffed quietly to himself, telepathically wishing her luck.

He sat gazing out of the window, watching the street below. A middle-aged woman whose ample curves had been compressed into a tight red dress was tottering on the pavement with a broken shoe heel. Her movements amused him, and he briefly forgot his depressed recriminations. For a second, he debated whether he should invite her inside whilst he fixed her shoe, but decided against it and continued to watch her until she hobbled out of view.

By mid-morning the following day, Hammond's head was threatening to burst. The team briefing had been postponed so he had spent the previous hours filtering through statements from people who had come forward with information. Many had simply confirmed they had visited Langdon Bay the day before the bodies had been discovered, but so far, no-one had reported seeing anything suspicious or had anything to offer that could launch the investigation into a hunt for a suspected perpetrator.

DCI Hunt had not shared with the team all the intelligence he had revealed to Hammond. The secrecy seemed unnecessary to Hammond; he couldn't see what Hunt hoped to gain from keeping quiet, but he was used to it. Lack of communication between departments, or even officers working on different shifts, had created numerous misunderstandings and unnecessary complications in the past. Several days earlier Hammond had learned of a sergeant working with POLSA who had deployed a search for a missing person, only to discover that the misper had been at home, having been found hours earlier by another officer. Good communication amongst officers was the foundation of any strong investigation, yet the simplest task of updating progress was considered to be too time consuming. In this sense, police work was like marriage; it was often the complacency that caused trouble.

He was startled when Dunn suddenly appeared in the doorway. Hammond glanced at her in greeting and was immediately struck by how she looked different from usual. He stared at her for several minutes, unsure what is was that made her appearance more distinguishable. He recognised the blouse and trousers she wore as her being her usual professional attire, but she seemed more... Hammond swallowed as he realised what it was. Dunn looked more pert than usual. Suddenly aware that he was gawping at her chest, he swung his gaze to the folder she was holding out to him.

"The post-mortem reports," she said as explanation. "DCI Hunt is occupied giving statements to the media. He's called for a team meeting in an hour."

He thanked her and took the folder from her outstretched hand, feeling slightly awkward as he did so, acutely embarrassed by his lecherous display. She left him to browse the material.

When the report had been issued, the bodies found on the beach had not been formally identified. The victims had been restrained, and therefore there were no defence marks on the bodies. Three of the victims had irregular and contuse oval entry wounds, measuring 25mm on the right side of the neck on one, and to the side of the head on two others. There was evidence of powder particles in the cavities. The soft tissue in the neck had hemorrhage with trauma to the right external carotid artery and jugular vein.

A muzzle imprint on the upper medial part of the right side of the neck was evident on one victim, with superficial cuts above and below this injury. The wounds on three of the victims were practically identical, indicating that they had been killed with the same weapon. No projectile or fragments of a projectile were discovered during the radiologic examination.

The fourth victim had depressed fractures to the back of the skull, with fragments of skull casing embedded in the brain. Residues of chalk dust and marine plant matter were observed near the impact site.

Hammond read through the report several times.

"Nasty," he said to himself, stating the obvious. The ferocity of the attacks indicated a hate crime – an execution driven by rage, or revenge. Hammond couldn't guess the killer's motivation, but whoever it was, they needed to be apprehended and quickly. He sighed deeply and stretched his arms behind his back. Much as he wanted the madman caught, he wasn't feeling optimistic.

He reviewed his last thought and wondered whether a woman could have committed the crime, so read the report again and concluded it was possible. Women were unpredictable creatures, especially the mad ones. His mind turned to Dunn; she certainly had altered lately. *Why was she looking so different?* He wondered if she was wearing figure-enhancing underwear in order to impress Hunt. Dunn was young, in her early thirties, still available. He wondered whether Hunt was gay; Hammond couldn't tell. The problem is, Hammond told himself, all women look great when they are blooming with youth. When they're single, their sex appeal is magnetic and exciting enough to snare their mate, but then they have children and the weight piles on and the libido diminishes. At least, it was that way with most women, excluding his ex-wife. Lyn hadn't lost her appeal. Hammond tried to remember what she had been like during the latter years of their marriage, but then wondered whether he had been so occupied with his work that he simply hadn't noticed her.

Two minutes before Hammond was due at the team debriefing, Hammond's mobile rang. He gave a start when he realised it was his son, and hastened to answer.

"Paul, I thought you had given up on me!" As soon as the words slipped out, he regretted them.

"Ditto." The voice at the other end sounded apathetic.

Ahead of Hammond, members of the team were filing through the doorway of the briefing room. He bit his lip, wanting to ask Paul to call back later, but didn't dare lose the only opportunity he had to make up for his insensitivity days earlier.

"I am very pleased to hear from you." Hammond spoke honestly. "How are you?"

There was a pause at the other end and he imagined his son shrugging as he answered, "Good, thanks. I was wondering if I could come and see you."

The surge of relief showed itself in an impromptu grin as Hammond replied, "Of course! You don't have to ask. When?"

Hunt had appeared at the end of the corridor, talking earnestly to Morris. Hammond edged his way closer to the briefing room, hoping he could end the conversation with discretion without appearing uninterested in his son's offer of a reunion.

He hastily offered a compromise. "Look, son, I'm really sorry but I'm supposed to go in a meeting. How about I get us a curry tomorrow night?". When none came, he threw in a bribe. "Bring a friend, if you like."

There was slight hesitation before Paul's voice rang clear with a new tone of enthusiasm. "I'll bring my girlfriend, you'll like her." Then the conversation was cut off.

In the seconds before Hunt entered the room, Hammond had shot in and pulled up a chair, giving the illusion he had been waiting several minutes. The only indication that Hammond had something other than work on his mind was the grin that looked as if it had been hoisted up by his ears.

CHAPTER SEVEN

"Good afternoon, everyone. Thank you for coming." Hunt addressed the expectant team as Morris closed the door and was the last to sit down. His long, outstretched legs rested directly against the legs of Hammond's chair, causing Hammond to wobble slightly. Morris greeted Hammond with a silent nod as Hunt set up his laptop to project the post-mortem photographs onto the whiteboard.

"You have all read the post-mortem notes, so you will all be aware that three of our victims were shot; two in the head, one in the neck, rupturing the major blood vessels and causing significant blood loss. The fact that there are muzzle imprints clearly defined on this victim..." He highlighted one of the images which depicted a close-up of an entry wound. "... confirms three were deliberately injured or killed with the use of a firearm." Hunt stopped to face his audience directly. "There was no trajectory of a bullet inside the brain, which suggests they were shot at close range using a blank firing gun."

Edwards swore quietly, but Hammond had heard his reaction and understood why the other man was concerned. Gun crime had reduced significantly during the last four years, following Kent Police's gun amnesty in 2008 which had encouraged the voluntary surrender of firearms without the fear of prosecution. It had been a success with many semi-automatics, shotguns, and automatics being taken off the street, but the huge amount of weapons confiscated had made it apparent that the availability of firearms was easier than had originally been supposed. A clean, unused 9mm automatic or a Glock could be bought for a couple of grand, while a sawn-off shotgun, preferred by the less sophisticated criminal, could be ordered for as little as £150. For street credibility, a self-loading pistol or an Uzi submachine gun could be ordered on any street in most British cities.

The last two years had seen an influx of firearms coming in from Eastern Europe – some sourced by former serviceman who had served in Afghanistan or Iraq. But, just like any business, the trends in firearms were driven by suppliers. It was easier and more profitable to export legal, blank-firing imitation pistols from Germany, which were then converted. Would-be gangsters wanted to be armed with less expensive and more readily available weaponry. Shotguns were too big and too heavy – the sawn-off looked clumsy; a machine gun was intimidating to enemies but wasn't discreet.

Hence, converted imitation guns were making up the highest proportion of recorded offences, especially amongst the younger, novice criminals. All that was needed was a drill press, a drill bit for the chamber, and another for the barrel in order to shoot 9mm rounds. But it required skill. Starter pistols were made purely to produce noise, using little more than cap-gun powder to make a loud bang. They were not made to fire live ammunition. The metal was too fragile to withstand the increased pressure needed to project a missile. It would take expertise to remove the partially blocked barrel and replace it with a rifled barrel, which was longer and threaded to allow an added silencer. Without the knowledge or the expertise, attempting to modify a blank firing gun would be as foolhardy as wrapping both hands around a grenade without a pin.

Hunt had also heard Edward's muffled response and was quick to correct the man's presumption. "There was no foreign projectile in the head and no exit wound, therefore it is un-likely that the starter pistol had been modified in any way. The gas pressure created when firing a blank pistol directly against the targets was, in this case, enough to demonstrate similar characteristics of a penetrating projectile."

Hunt's eyes turned away from Edwards as he addressed the whole team.

"However, this gives us valuable information on our perpetrator. One, our killer is inexperienced and naive. We know this because he or she had expected to execute all victims in the same manner, without understanding the characteristics of the weapon they were using. Two, the sadism shown in the killing indicates that our killer is emotionally involved. This was not a professional hit. When the pistol failed to kill the young male, our killer lost their temper and resorted to beating them to death using a stone. This was an amateurish and careless move, and one that required intimacy of contact. Beating someone to death isn't quick, and it requires physical exertion. There is a chance that we will find trace fibres, the killer's saliva or sweat. Human vomit was found near the steps heading back. It could be our killer's, especially if they were overwhelmed with adrenalin following the attacks."

Edwards nodded as Hunt spoke. He interjected, "So, what you are saying is that it is likely these murders were a personal attack? Someone with a grudge? Possibly a younger, less experienced assailant with an obvious motive?"

"Obvious only to the killer, I suspect," Morris said. "Otherwise, to us and to everyone, it looks a motive-less crime driven by hate."

Dunn added, "A race-hate crime possibly?"

Hunt spread his hands with open palms, a neutral gesture to compensate for a non-definitive answer. "We must use this information to our advantage. We now know that these murders were poorly planned. They were intentional, but they were not carried out by a professional killer. For the sake of practicality, let's assume we are looking for a perpetrator working alone, until we can prove otherwise." He paused and turned the projector off. The room grew instantly darker.

Hunt stood, looking down at the floor for several seconds. Hammond automatically followed the man's gaze. The light coming from the window reflected off the sheen of Hunt's alligator leather shoes. The man had class, Hammond had to credit the man for that.

Hunt continued, "The information we have gathered from the post-mortems alone tells us we are dealing with an experimentalist. This means there may be more deaths, more planned executions."

There was increased activity for several minutes as the team deliberated over their investigation. They revised the findings of the forensic team. The technicians had checked fingerprints from the handrail on the cliff path and compared them with the national database, but the job was extensive and unlikely to produce useful results. Thousands of visitors had used the path in recent days, so it would be near impossible to identify the culprit's prints amongst so many others. Secondly, it had rained the night before the killings, which meant evidence could have been compromised. Thirdly, the scene was constantly changing with the incoming tide; any clues had probably been washed away by the time the forensic examination had commenced.

The plastic tree ties removed from the victims' wrists by the coastguard had been examined for any trace evidence. No unaccounted prints had been found, which suggested the killer had worn gloves. Dunn had been occupied researching any known criminals with records of assault in the local area. Edwards had interviewed local residents, regular visitors to the area, nearby campsites, and staff at the nearest visitor centre. Hammond had revised every detail of each report. There was not much to go on, but he clung onto the hope that sooner or later something would come up, it was just a matter of time.

"Our priority is to identify the victims," Hunt went on. "We are awaiting further findings, but in the meantime, we must interview the surviving victim. She is our only witness.

As soon as she is conscious, we must talk to her. In the mean-time, focus on the motive. Our victims could have been killed in quicker, more effective ways. Why the clumsy application of torture?"

By now, Hunt had sat himself on the edge of the desk. One leg was crossed over the other at the ankle, his trousers slightly hitched up at the knee, showing yellow socks with distinctive blue stripes.

"Desperation?" Dunn spoke up, her hand brushing an invisible strand of hair from the side of her brow. "It could have been related to drugs or money. Desperation to gain or to retrieve information."

Dover had seen a rapid acceleration of drug-related crime in the last decade. Within the last four weeks, over 300 crimes had been reported in one area of the town, mostly anti-social or violent behaviour, but drug dependency had been in the background for almost all of them.

"The killer wanted the murders to be recognised as an execution," Hammond said. "In our killer's eyes, the victims had committed a crime. If the killer had wanted something from them, shooting the starter gun above their heads would have been loud enough to create fear. They were going to die regardless."

Hunt nodded in agreement, then addressed Dunn. "There's no residue of drugs or chemicals to suggest they were drug mules... and the methodology seems too haphazard. A drug-related killing would be more sophisticated, surely?" He looked defeated for several seconds before pushing himself off the desk with renewed enthusiasm. "Let's stick with what we do know and work with that. Our killer knew the victims, or was involved with them. They knew the victims would be at the place at that time; they anticipated the tide patterns. They have local knowledge of the area, or have been at the area before whilst planning the event. It's something personal. If our killer is racially biased, chances are we will find they have shown racist behaviour in the past. Look at all records of assault, abuse, anything that has been targeted against foreigners or migrants. Go through any witness accounts that suggest someone in the vicinity displaying odd behaviour in the last few days or weeks."

Dunn had left the room with the rest of the team when Hunt turned to Hammond. His eyes pierced Hammond with an intensity the other man found un-nerving. "I just hope we find the perpetrator before he kills again."

The call from the officer stationed at the hospital informed them that the female patient was awake just before six, and it was decided that Dunn would accompany Hammond to the hospital. They drove the quicker route along the motorway and parked by the ambulance bay.

The woman was sitting up in bed, looking out the window. The view was compromised by the ebbing light outside, yet she did not notice Hammond and Dunn's arrival until he uttered a discreet sound to gain her attention. She gave a start and turned her head towards him as he introduced himself and DS Lois Dunn.

The woman's eyes were sunken, with a haunted expression. With her mouth tightly closed, she gave no indication of understanding him. For a second, Hammond panicked. *Did she understand English? What language did they speak in Ethiopia, if that was indeed where she had come from? Arabic? Somali?* He looked sideways at Dunn, hoping for her to be able to relate as a woman, but she simply smiled and allowed him to take the lead.

"*Parlez-vous français?*" He attempted to remember his schoolboy French, aware of his bad pronunciation.

The woman continued to look at him, still silent. A crease appeared between her brows before she gave a slight indication of her head.

Shit. The idea of attempting to converse in a language he couldn't speak well was intolerable.

"*Nous suis* detectives." He used his hand to elaborate unnecessarily whilst he floundered, searching his memory for any French expressions he could think of that could help.

"*Nous voulons vous aider. Quel est votre nom?*"

Again, the woman nodded. She looked at Dunn, still silent, whilst Hammond turned to his colleague.

"Can't you help?" he hissed.

"Try your phone. Retrieve a language app whilst we wait for a translator."

"I can speak English." The woman's voice beckoned his attention back to the bed.

"Oh. Why didn't you say earlier?"

"You asked if I spoke French. I speak French and English."

Feeling his face redden slightly, he gestured to the chair, as if seeking permission to sit beside the bed. Dunn remained standing.

"So, you understand that we are detectives and we are here to help you? To find out who hurt you and why?"

"Yes. But my memory is not so good." She raised her hand to the side of her face, gently touching the dressings that now covered the burnt flesh.

"Can you tell me your name?"

Despite his gentle tone, the woman seemed nervous and reluctant to answer. Dunn stepped forward.

"You are not in trouble. We just need to understand what happened to you." She offered a reassuring smile.

"My name is Asli. I am allowed to stay in England. I am legal."

"You were found near Langdon Bay. Can you tell us what you were doing there?"

"I am legal." The one eye that wasn't swollen showed a hint of moisture.

Hammond leaned forward. "I believe you, Asli. I am not here to accuse you. I want to find out how you got hurt."

The woman turned away from him, her gaze returning to the window. She remained silent.

Hammond reached into his inner pocket and withdrew photos of the victims found on Langdon Bay. He gently arranged them on the bedcovers and waited for her to look at them. When she did, the fear was now more apparent on her face.

"Asli. I do not want to frighten you. You are safe here and you can talk to me without fear. I really do want to help you. Do you understand?" He waited for a sign of acknowledgement before he continued. "These people were found near you. They had also been hurt. Did you know them?"

The photographs were looked at for several silent seconds, then she looked up at Hammond.

"I wanted to help them. I promised them they would be safe with me."

No more words were said. Asli had turned her back to them. The interview was over.

The drive back to the station was tense. Hammond was irritated with Dunn. She was the first to get upset if she was not given the opportunity to contribute in interviews, yet she had more or less taken a back seat whilst Hammond had struggled. He had needed her to gain the trust from another woman, but instead he had blundered in carelessly and caused the woman to clam up. The information they had gathered was not enough to help them progress in the investigation.

"We'll start by contacting immigration in the morning to verify her residential status," he said. "If she was telling the truth, there will be records that may lead us to the identity of the other victims."

"You think it is plausible that she wasn't trying to sneak into the UK? I doubt we will find any granted application for asylum under her name."

"It's one thing to be suspicious, Dunn, quite another to lack hope."

Hammond turned into the car park. It was beginning to get dark, and the threat of a wet night hovered over them.

SHOES ON A WIRE

"So, that's what our investigations are reliant on now, is it? Hope?" Dunn's voice was rich in sarcasm. She stepped out of the car and reached back in to retrieve her bag.

Despite his annoyance, Hammond smiled broadly. "Before every achievement, there was hope to achieve it, surely?"

"If you say so." Dunn offered a wave of her hand before she headed back to her own car, parked nearby. "I'll see you in the morning. Maybe a miracle will happen tomorrow." Her voice was anything but positive, yet Hammond smiled at her retreating back.

"That's the spirit!"

CHAPTER EIGHT

Wallace Hammond was awoken by the sound of torrential rain battering the windows. He fumbled in the half light for his mobile phone resting on the dresser beside him, and blinked as the screen showed him it was twenty past five. It was not the ideal start to a Saturday morning. He got up, not bothering to put on his dressing gown, and opened the curtains to survey the scene outside. The contrast between the shadow in his bedroom and the mirrored light dancing on the wet streets below compelled him to open the window and breathe in the freshness of the air outside.

He found himself blinking from the rain that splashed onto his face and into his eyes as it rebounded from the window ledge, but he remained where he was, allowing his gaze to sweep from east to west as he considered why he had settled in the town of Folkestone rather than anywhere else. He wouldn't have chosen the town as his home if he had not been divorced. It was too noisy and there were many areas he would avoid wandering around on his own at night, but it was cheaper to live here than in the surrounding smaller towns. In some select areas, it was attractive, especially the old high street with its cobbled roads leading down towards the harbour. There had been rumours several years ago that the harbour was to be rebuilt as a marina and there had, from what Hammond could tell, been developments, with new housing, shops, and a small university campus. But the recession and the influx of immigrants had compromised the grand masterplan to reinvent Folkestone as a desirable place to live.

Below him, Hammond noticed a street cleaner starting his shift, picking up the takeaway wrappers and bottles that had been discarded carelessly by the usual Friday night pub crawlers. He watched the man for several minutes, before leaving history and the town's inhabitants to their own devices and headed for the shower.

Hammond's first task when he reached the station was to check for any updates on the missing mother. To his disappointment, there had been no reports of anyone searching for a lost new born infant, not had there been any information from the local hospitals on childless women showing signs of recent childbearing. The baby's origins remained a mystery; the media had lost interest and Morris had stopped asking for any updates. There was no missing person report that could be connected. Everyone except Hammond appeared to have forgotten all about the infant, he surmised, before heading for the coffee machine.

Several minutes later, revived by a sweet coffee and a cereal bar, Hammond had better news awaiting him in his e-mail messages. Forensics had identified foreign DNA on the male victim who had been beaten. Later, it would be compared to any suspects or former perpetrators in the database. It was unlikely there would be any progress during the weekend, and it was reliant on the chance that the offender had previously committed a crime, but it was an encouraging development nonetheless.

He scanned his inbox for additional information and was disappointed to read an update from SOCO that the cliff path leading to Langdon Bay had collapsed overnight, due to the heavy rainfall. It wasn't a total disaster, since the path had been processed as thoroughly as was possible beforehand, but it would mean any attempts to recreate the event for the benefit of potential witnesses was now improbable.

DS Lois Dunn had done her homework. Immigration had confirmed Asli Rahim had been granted asylum the previous year, and since then had been employed as a residential care worker in Deal. There was limited information available on the woman's background. She had stated she was from Somalia. Rebels had ambushed her home village, and she had fled the massacre as a child. That was the only information she had been willing to give, other than that she had been arrested in Scotland, suspected of obtaining false documents to stay in the country. It was possible, the report stated, that Asli had been honest in her account, but since many asylum seekers use false identities or elaborated their circumstances to aid their application, it could not be confirmed one way or other.

Asli had shown great promise in her willingness to learn English and learn a trade, therefore asylum had been granted with the necessary conditions. It was evident, reading the sketchy intelligence that Dunn had gathered, that Asli had reason to be concerned. If there was any hint of her being involved in the killings on Langdon Bay, she would be deported.

Hammond sighed. He was well aware of the resentment caused by immigrants taking up space in the country. He himself wondered if the country would be in a better place financially and morally if there were less allowances made for foreigners taking up residence and employment in Britain. Yet at the same time, he took pride in his country for allowing sanctuary to those in desperate need; everyone had the right to feel safe, to have a home, to have a life.

Hammond deliberated. If our country was falling apart around us, we would be looking for somewhere to run. The human race is supposed to have evolved, yet we are snarling at each other like primitives trying to protect our territories. It would be easier to pee on a tree like an animal to avoid turf wars. There was a time when criminal gangs marked their territories by hanging shoes on telephone wires; it had begun as a sign showing where drugs could be bought, but the meaning had evolved into something more threatening.

Urban myths told that shoes thrown over power lines had been taken from trespassers venturing into criminal territories.

It was ironic to think that one of the victims on the beach had no shoes on when he was found. A coincidence maybe, or maybe a reference to the crime the victim had committed. Perhaps he had entered another territory illegally and been punished as a consequence. Hammond's thoughts were becoming unfocused and erratic. He finished his coffee and shut down the computer. There wasn't much more investigating that could be done until Monday, but in the meantime, there was something he needed to do.

For just over three hours, Hammond had tried his best to gain the trust of the young woman seated opposite him. His offering of a basket-weaving kit "to remind her of home and to help pass the time" was a clumsy attempt to appear friendly, but Asli had accepted his gift with a gracious inclination of her head. Since then, he had mainly talked about himself, his family, even snippets from his childhood. He hoped that he would be accepted, not as a man, but as a human who simply wanted to offer her justice and accept her help in return.

She had acknowledged his explanation, but she remained reluctant to talk about herself or the events leading up to their meeting. Eventually, Hammond had run out of things to say. He was painfully aware that he had been talking the whole time, but was reassured by her apparent interest.

Asli had improved since the previous day. She was eating and sipping water, her wounds looked clean, and there was less doubt that they would heal entirely. The psychological damage would take longer, Hammond knew that. But if there was a way to reassure her, he wanted to find it. His patience worked. Just before visiting hours came to an end, Asli asked to look at the photographs of the victims again. He obliged, keeping silent whilst she focused on the images before her.

"Sakina had been pregnant with her first child; she had placenta disruption and would have died if she had not received emergency medical aid. Afterwards, she could not go home. She feared her husband would kill her if he knew she had exposed herself to a male doctor. She told me her sister Mahgul had been executed by her brother-in-law following allegations of adultery, even though the girl had been too young and too sheltered to have been alone with another man. Sakina fled Afghanistan with the promise she would be safe in England."

Hammond looked at the image of the female victim. "She told you this?"

Asli nodded her head.

"What else did she tell you?"

"Not much. It is hard to know who to trust, but I think I reminded her of her sister."

"You tried to help her?"

"Yes."

"How? Did you arrange a way for her to come over to England?"

"No. I met her before she travelled. I helped by being a friend to her."

The last comment was empty of meaning, but Hammond ignored it for the time being. "You met her somewhere else?"

Asli didn't reply, but simply nodded. Despite the urge to persuade her to give more information, Hammond couldn't risk pressuring her, so instead he waited. His eardrums reverberated with the thumping of his quickening heart.

"Do you know her last name?"

"No." The answer was prompt, signaling the reluctance to divulge too much. Hammond knew he was running out of time.

"What about the others? What can you tell me about them?"

Asli's finger pointed out the younger male; she had noticed the missing shoes. Her features tightened before she met Hammond's gaze.

"This one, I met him before also. I do not know his name, but I can give you an address. I know where he was staying in France before he came here."

Hammond smiled, showing his appreciation. "And the others?"

She shook her head. "No. I cannot tell you any more."

Hammond waited for her to write the address in his notebook before thanking her. "Asli, your help is greatly appreciated. I do understand you are frightened, and I wish I could tell you that I can protect you from being deported if the authorities believe you have acted illegally and are somehow responsible for those people arriving in Dover covertly. But I can't until I know everything. Do you understand?" He waited for her to signal her understanding.

Satisfied with a nod, he continued, "If there is anything you can tell me, anything to help to find justice for Sakina and the others, it will be noted. The more you can co-operate, the better it will be for you."

Asli looked at him intently as if she were measuring his sincerity. "I wanted to help others who had nowhere to run. I was helped by a good man when I needed somewhere to run, too. Now I try to do the same for others."

Hammond frowned. "You work alone, or for someone else?"

Asli shook her head slowly, Hammond could see she was reluctant to divulge, but she was intelligent enough to know her story would be checked out and her co-operation could only help her. "Please understand, my employer is a good man. He pays me well to look after his elderly mother; she has dementia so needs constant care, but sometimes I am asked to do other work, like liaising with boat owners to arrange transport of people who do not have travel documents. Sometimes I help with translating, but that is all."

Hammond had the details of her employer at the office, so he did not pressure her for more details. The sound of scraping chairs and cheery goodbyes in the ward outside signaled the end of visiting hours.

"What happened to you, Asli?" Hammond's tone was gentle and sympathetic, offering her the opportunity to defend herself. But it was evident she wasn't ready to accept.

"You will come again?"

"Yes." Hammond wanted to add the condition that she would give him more information, but he held back.

"Maybe next time I will tell you my story." Asli smiled, exposing bright large teeth, and Hammond recognised the first glimmer of hope.

Wallace Hammond always looked forward to his son's visits. They did not happen as often as he would have liked, so he had anticipated the evening with enthusiasm. The apartment had been cleaned, the still unopened wedding invitation retrieved from the front mat and moved to the kitchen windowsill, the carpet vacuumed. The take-away curry had been chosen with care. Five main courses, two rice options, and several side orders, had been expensive, but it was better to order too much than not offer enough choice.

The beers were chilled, and everything had been organised with the intention of creating a welcoming and homely atmosphere. It was natural that Hammond was slightly nervous. The relationship between his son and himself had been strained since his divorce from Paul's mother, but this was the first time the boy had been willing to introduce his father to a girlfriend. It was a sign that Paul wanted to include his father in his life as much as Hammond did.

When the apartment's buzzer indicated their arrival, Hammond sprang up with eagerness to answer the door. But upon doing so, he immediately stopped short. Two thoughts instantly flashed through his mind: the first was that Paul appeared incredibly short; the second was that Paul had brought a long-lost aunt with him, one that Hammond had never met, instead of his girlfriend. He gaped at the towering woman standing before him.

"Dad, this is Bettina."

Hammond offered his hand automatically, but shot a glance at Paul standing behind her. Was Paul teasing him? Apparently not. As Paul ushered the woman forward, he was beaming with pride, his eyes not wavering from the giant of the woman who was now entering the apartment and clasping Hammond's hand with a firm grip.

He stammered a greeting and followed them into the living room, using the opportunity to study Paul's guest from behind. He noted the strands of grey in Bettina's otherwise brunette hair; her stride equaled her almost masculine demeanor. Muscular calves were evident beneath a knee-length skirt, and the cotton blouse she wore was unflattering for her broad shoulders, contributing to a frumpy, tired appearance. Hammond estimated the woman looked no younger than her mid-forties.

He arranged his features into a smile as she turned to face him, and offered her a drink, all the while talking nonsense as he attempted to regain his composure. Having settled them and left them to talk amongst themselves, he retreated to the kitchen and leaned on the back of the kitchen chair. *What the hell was his son thinking? Or rather*, he corrected himself, *what was that woman thinking, dating a man half her age?*

The evening did not progress smoothly. Despite Hammond's resolve to appear friendly, it quickly became apparent that Bettina was astute. She had noted Hammond's shock and was determined to make him suffer for his initial prejudice. She answered his polite questioning with a defensive manner, hinting towards arrogance, as she explained she was a lecturer of Gender Studies and had been a guest speaker in International Politics at City University in London. She had met Paul there two years ago, when he was studying Computer Science.

Hammond's expression revealed his surprise; *they couldn't have been together that long without him knowing, surely?*

Paul nodded, smiling. It was evident the lad was smitten. Hammond hadn't seen his son look so happy in a long time, and there was little point in asking if they were a serious couple. The realization that he had missed so much of Paul's life swamped him with a despair that he found difficult to hide. He distracted himself by helping himself to Chicken Madras, dipping his chapatti into the thick sauce, forgetting to mind his table manners.

"So, how's work? Caught any criminals lately?" Paul offered his father the opportunity to talk about himself.

Hammond shrugged, reluctant to discuss work when he had been given this rare opportunity to spend time with family and guests.

"I heard about the bodies washed up at Dover. Are you involved?"

Hammond nodded without enthusiasm. "Yes, I am part of the investigative team. I can't give details, though, mainly because we don't have much more information than the media."

"They were immigrants." Bettina spoke factually rather than posing a question.

"Possibly."

"Undoubtedly. Probably trying to sneak onto British soil undetected." Bettina leaned forward and took another onion bhaji from the plate offered. "This country is too lenient. The British may as well have enormous signs flashing from the Dover cliffs saying 'Welcome, help yourselves'."

"I hardly think that's the case," Hammond replied, noting Paul's amusement at Bettina's statement.

"Of course it is! Within decades, the British white caucasian will be a minority. We have over 200,000 Roma migrants resident in the UK, and there are more to come. Meanwhile, they are filling our hospitals and our schools, expecting us to respect their cultural or religious lifestyles whilst getting paid benefits so they can stay at home whilst the British nationals are paying the price."

She was antagonizing him. Hammond should have kept quiet or changed the subject, but her comment had irritated him. "I am sure your opinion is shared, Bettina, but some would argue that the more people who contribute to British society, the better the collective benefit to Britain's economy and the welfare state that depends on it. Skilled professional immigrants, who bring their expertise into Britain, can be a huge advantage."

Bettina snorted in reply. She grinned at Paul seated beside her, as if to include him in the debate, but he seemed to be in awe of her dominance and remained silent. His eyes never left her as she launched further into the debate.

"That could only be the opinion of a middle-class, left-wing minority, wanting to appear superior. Working class families will suffer most from what will become a failed multicultural society." Bettina leaned forward again as she continued. "Civil unrest of unimaginable proportions will be the inevitable consequence of the deliberate destruction of British culture caused by left-leaning Labour, Conservative, and coalition governments." She ended the sentence by biting on a poppadom with enough gusto to cause a glob of mango chutney to plop off the end onto the table.

"So, as an educated woman, what do you suggest could prevent this destruction of British culture?"

Bettina shot a suspicious glance at Hammond, but he appeared genuinely interested in her answer. "Integration will only work if British culture and British ways are first acknowledged and respected. Instead of allowing the migrants into our society immediately, segregate to educate. Show them how to be British."

Paul was nodding enthusiastically at Bettina's words. "Exactly, the only reason why there is opposition to immigration is because the majority of foreigners do not respect our laws or our religions," he chipped in. "They beg, cluster around gambling venues, and dump rubbish in the streets. It's blatant disrespect which we are opposed to."

"Who's we?" Hammond's irritation was evident in the tone of his voice. He found Bettina's attitude ignorant and was surprised by how easily led Paul was being. There was a time when Paul had had a mind of his own.

Paul looked at his father quizzically, surprised by the question. "The majority."

"Hasn't history shown us how segregating and highlighting cultural differences contributes to nothing more than discrimination?"

"Of course not! Bloody hell, Dad! Why the attitude?" Paul was flushed, embarrassed by his father's apparent lack of interest in their political debate.

Bettina leaned towards Hammond, her eyebrows raised with indignation.

"Defending white British homogeneity is not an act of racism; it is simply expressing a preference to retain what makes us proud to be British. If anything, it is the immigrants who refuse to welcome strangers or cultural differences in their home countries. *They* behave as intolerant racist or religious radicals!"

Hammond had had enough. The evening had turned into a farce. He stood up and began collecting the empty plates. He was aware his face was reddening and his irritation threatened to burst forth with a rude comment. Somehow, he managed to restrain himself and retreated to the kitchen leaving Bettina and Paul to chat to each other.

CHAPTER NINE

Hammond had never attempted to meditate. But in his opinion, attending a strategy revision meeting with members of the Kent Police Authority was as close to the real thing. It was an activity he felt he had no right to be involved in. Hammond was not allowed to contribute suggestions, merely to make up numbers of bums on seats, so cognitive demands were exempt. But circumstances had dictated that he was at the bidding of Acting Superintendent Morris, hence he was here, listening to the long-winded speeches instead of his boss.

Hammond was well aware he was being kept away from the office whilst DCI Hunt was briefing Europol, but the one positive outcome of being delegated the task was that it was another reminder of the disadvantages of promotion. A higher salary and more annual holidays were the perks, but it was overshadowed by increased paperwork and the stress of managing crime statistics and departmental budgets – exactly why Hammond had never aspired to climbing the ranks.

Intermittently, between bouts of monotone explanations and white noise, he was conscious of subjects changing. According to the clock on the wall, the latest topic – expenditure in forensics – had taken over 40 minutes, and yet there seemed to be no conclusion to the proposal of budget cuts being switched to another department.

Hammond had resisted the urge to suggest ceasing all meaningless meetings to cut back on filtered coffee for independent members, but instead concentrated on what he would do next. He intended to meet Asli's employer, but wanted to question the woman again and get his facts straight regarding her work placement before blundering in and raising hackles.

He was surprised to realise that he was looking forward to seeing Asli again. Her gentle tone and expressive eyes were appealing, but it was her story that attracted him more. It was difficult to comprehend the life she had endured. The dramatic events Asli had experienced were almost implausible; the plot stolen from a movie, yet it was real. And as such, Hammond felt out of his depth in how to deal with her.

She had information that could prove crucial to the investigation, yet Hammond was aware that one false move on his part could jeopardise the trust he had established and the information could be withheld. Such a consequence could sabotage the police's chances of a conviction by the guilty party, but Hammond's apprehension was morally based. Asli needed to see that she was cared for, that she was not surrounded by enemies in every corner. And if he could, Hammond wanted to convince her that the human race had some good people left in it.

The meeting dragged on for another half hour before he was able to check his messages. There were several missed calls, and a voicemail from DCI Hunt requesting his presence. The recorded message was rich in arrogance, which only succeeded in making Hammond take his time to reach the office where Hunt was waiting.

"I have not heard much to suggest we are making any progress." DCI Hunt's attention was entirely focused on Hammond, who sat opposite him at the desk feeling like a schoolboy about to be reprimanded.

"So far, our focus has been on identifying the victims. We've got two names and an address overseas. Our surviving witness, Asli Rahim, is offering information tentatively; we have a connection and a sketchy outline of the circumstances leading to their deaths. She knew the victims. There was the suggestion that her official employment as a resident carer is a front for other work involving communicating with boat owners to arrange transportation of immigrants. It appears she is aware of their covert entry into England, because she translates for them. However, it is a slow process. I have not questioned her as a suspect yet."

Hunt interrupted. "Why? She is our only lead at this time. We need to get on with accumulating and applying intelligence."

Hammond agreed. "However, sir, on this occasion I feel that enforcing pressure on Asli will be detrimental. She is traumatised by her ordeal, so if we push her too hard, she may clam up entirely."

"That is not for you to decide. Unless you are a trained psychologist specializing in mental trauma, you are not qualified to decide what is best for her. It is your job to retrieve information as quickly and as efficiently as possible. If necessary, liaise through the social workers. Do you think she could be involved with the killer?"

"She has suggested she was involved with bringing the victims to Dover, but she seemed genuinely shocked by their deaths. There is a sense of guilt on her part, so she is possibly guilty of a crime but not murder."

Hunt's eyebrows rose. He paused for several seconds whilst he studied Hammond intently, causing him to redden under the scrutiny.

"Is there a chance that Asli was employed under deception? That she was offered work as a carer, but it was simply a way of exploiting her skills for illegal employment?"

Hammond gestured the possibility with a raised shoulder. "Possibly, but she is an intelligent woman. Vulnerable or otherwise, I don't think she could be so easily manipulated."

Hunt referred to the papers spread before him on the desk. "According to your report, you stated that Asli said, quote: 'I was helped by a good man when I needed somewhere to run to. Now I try to do the same for others.' Unquote. That indicates two possibilities: One, Asli has affection for her employer. Two, that she is indebted to them. Both are tools for manipulation."

Hammond agreed. "From what I understood, Asli showed respect for her employer, rather than affection."

"Respect for another suggests admiration, even in its mildest form. Therefore, she appears open to influence, which could also mean she may have consented to employment but under deception, hence her evidence could lean this investigation more heavily onto trafficking."

Hammond's discomfort was increasing. The implications of trafficking meant their investigation was likely to become huge. It wouldn't be just the Major Crime Team's responsibility but several other syndicates as well. That would mean longer delays to get results, not to mention a greater need to justify every action and every use of resources. In turn, that would mean more paperwork, more pressure, and a far greater chance of becoming the scapegoat further down in the ranks when, or if, the investigation proved fruitless. As if reading his thoughts, Hunt interjected.

"DI Hammond, I will be frank. I am aware that in the last few years you have lost a colleague in upsetting circumstances. You have also lost your home and nearly your life less than three years ago."

Hammond was unprepared for the change in topic. "That is true. However, it has not affected my ability to do my job."

"I disagree. I have looked at your file. In 2011, you were investigated by Professional Standards for entering a potential crime scene without an initial risk assessment, reinforcements or permission from your commanding officer, which possibly contributed to the murder of DC Michael Galvin. You've been known to withhold information from your team, and have been reprimanded on several occasions for acting independently during major investigations. Your commanding officer was DCI Beech during this time period?"

The blow struck Hammond hard in the gut. The death of DC Galvin had caused him many sleepless nights and endless bouts of guilt since, but he felt the need to defend any insinuation that he had ever perjured himself.

"DCI Beech was a good officer. He would not have tolerated faked evidence or biased investigations. He knew I wanted to complete any investigation to the best of my ability, despite limited resources or manpower. I should also point out that Professional Standards did not hold me accountable for the death of DC Galvin."

Hammond's words were acknowledged with a hint of a smirk before Hunt continued. "I assume that despite DCI Beech's leniency, he was confident that despite your inadequacies, you found answers and were dedicated to apprehending guilty parties, even at the risk of sacrificing yourself or your career. Your methods are shoddy, you ignore procedure, your colleagues have described you as temperamental and obstinate. You are not a team player, which I cannot abide, but..." Hunt expressed a sigh to show his reluctance in what he was about to say "...but you get the job done. So, do what you do, find our killer by whatever means necessary, and I will turn a blind eye when necessary. Although note, I will not tolerate insubordination or underhand methods, and only until the perpetrator is charged and we have enough evidence to have him or her apprehended. I will not accept any behaviour that risks our chances of having a conviction."

Hunt leaned forward, resting his elbows of the desk with his hands clasped together. It made him look more like a teacher addressing a child.

"DCI Beech was a respected and well liked man. I am not interested in gaining admiration for being a nice man. I want any investigation I run to have a successful outcome. I want to be recognised as being an outstanding officer because what matters here is getting results. You get results, which is why I am prepared to support you. This witness..." Hunt's voice tailed off whilst he attempted to refresh his memory.

"Asli Rahim."

"Yes, her. Understand that there is pressure from all sides on this. I've been given the strictest orders to keep this investigation in-house until we know exactly what we are dealing with.

Border Force are keen to get involved, but we have been granted another day to interview Asli before the higher authorities take over, so I won't allow trading information for leniency. If she is guilty of a crime and there is evidence to prove it, we will charge her or hand her over. Either way, she has information about what happened on the beach, so we need to interview her officially as a suspect. Ask Dunn to prepare an interview strategy whilst you check out her employer, find out why he employed her, whether her work is supervised by a third party, identify anyone who can corroborate her story."

Hammond nodded. "There is of course, a chance that this could be gang-related. If our victims were not seeking refuge in England, but were involved in organizing transportation of immigrants, their deaths may be the result of a turf war between migrant gangs."

Hunt drew back his chair and rummaged in the briefcase leaning against the side of the desk before throwing a newspaper on the desk in front of Hammond.

"Have you seen this?

Hammond scanned the headline. *Ports re-opened in Libya; more migrants expected to flood Europe.*

He nodded. "I try to avoid the hype."

Hunt offered a noise resembling a snort and returned to his seat. "This is what we are up against; the newly porous borders in Libya mean we are now challenged with the migrant influx from numerous other areas, such as Eritrea or Sudan, as well as Afghanistan. Frontex recorded 42,000 migrants coming into this country within four months. There are at least 35 successful covert crossings over the Channel every day, and that doesn't include the attempted crossings or the deaths caused during the attempts. Bodies are being found in the Mediterranean and the English Channel on a regular basis.

"This is a huge deal, and the responsibility is marginally on our shoulders. If we make a wrong move on this investigation by false implications, or are seen to handle this investigation clumsily, we will become the scapegoats accused of enabling illegal migration. Or worse, will be regarded by the public we serve as racist bigots, and the media will waste no time in pointing the finger at our incompetence. Once the media start twisting facts, public hysteria will be the inevitable consequence, which ultimately we will have to diffuse."

Hunt paused for breath before adding, "God knows, we do not want this area to become known as another lawless jungle like Calais. The trust we have established with the communities we serve will be lost and will have to be built up all over again. We can't let that happen, Hammond. We must make an arrest within the next 48 hours to satisfy the ACC and the public that we are managing this investigation productively."

Hammond stretched his arms round the back of his chair. He felt heaviness on his chest that wasn't being relieved by the change of position. He understood the problem Hunt was foreseeing. Although the police were not responsible for the control of migrants entering the country illegally, it was now imperative for all authorities to work together.

Hunt was right; the situation in Calais was now infamously out of control, with riots breaking out on a daily basis, and French police resorting to using teargas and rubber bullets in an attempt to regain order. The migrants were in constant need of shelter, food, and medicine; hence the new permanent Jules Ferry camp had just been opened only a ten-minute walk from where the migrants jumped on lorries bound for the UK. A part of the annual £6million pound bill would be paid using a £3million 'special' grant from the EU that included money from British taxpayers.

Secretly, Hammond had no confidence in such progress; history was repeating itself. The holding camp at Sangatte had been built in 1999 with the intention to *solve* the problem of a mass influx of refugees into Britain, but had instead become a stepping stone for entry into the UK. So, the camp was closed, dismantled, and handed back to its landholder, Eurotunnel, in

2002. Now, only 12 years later, the situation was no different, other than the new holding camp provided meals cooked by a three-star Michelin chef.

The room became silent as both men considered the enormity of the task ahead. This wasn't simply a murder investigation any more. There were serious risks involved. The first was the public hysteria that Hunt was anticipating. If the media portrayed the killings as a racist or hate crime, there would be fear set within the local community which consisted of thousands of foreign nationals. Within the last 12 months, Kent Police had responded to numerous outbreaks of violence between those who wanted them out and those who wanted to continue practising their cultural traditions within Britain. Hammond sighed heavily. The situation was overwhelming.

Hunt looked at him sharply. "Of course, the situation could escalate even more now with this Ebola outbreak. So many African migrants are sneaking in, it is only a matter of time before Britain has an epidemic."

Hammond rose from his chair slowly, aware that his right knee clicked as he extended his leg. The atmosphere in the office was becoming unbearably depressing. "If these murders are politically orientated, it could be that the Ebola outbreak is a trigger; I'm stretching a theory somewhat, but we have agreed we are dealing with a murderer whose method of killing suggested a personal vendetta. The Ebola outbreak is the most recent in a string of media hype stories where blame is attributed to the integration of foreign societies. Maybe our killer has had a negative personal experience with a foreign national. This could be a revenge attack; a transference of rage against someone who had caused them harm in the past." Hammond's hands gestured enthusiastically as he allowed himself to think creatively.

He noted Hunt's look of scepticism and continued his thread quickly. "I know, it is a long shot, but we could look at victims of crime who have been targeted by foreigners, as well as searching for offenders who have been accused of attacking foreigners. I am not claiming to be a profiler here, but such crimes do occasionally show a pattern of behaviour. Homophobic murders have been committed by homosexual perpetrators ashamed of their sexual preferences, or sexually motivated crimes been committed by sexually abused victims reliving their past. It is not improbable that this case shows a similar pattern."

Hunt held up a hand, stopping Hammond's flow. "It is a long shot. I personally do not like being creative by theorising. I like to examine evidence and facts. However, there is not enough facts to lead us in one direction, so until then, I'll go along with your ideas. Look for previous victims as well as suspects, but don't spend too much time on possibilities. I admit, the idea appeals to me because it will show us to be less discriminate when we eventually make an arrest. However, stick to what we do have as priority. Interview Asli's employer before questioning her as a suspect. Follow where that leads us first."

Chapter Ten

Ostentatious displays of wealth normally had Hammond looking away repelled, but he had to admit he was secretly impressed as he waited for the electronic wooden gates to open and allow entry into the private grounds of Elm Cottage. Despite the name, the property was not a modest home. The car crunched over a gravel drive before arriving at a turning area paved in swept York stone and granite slabs.

As they exited the car, Edwards gestured towards the swimming pool slightly hidden behind structural beech hedging, interspersed with cherry trees. He gave a low whistle and raised his eyebrows.

"Wish the Missus could see this!"

Hammond declined to answer, aware of a stress ball forming in the pit of his stomach. He had always been secretly intimidated by wealthy people; their air of exclusivity tended to make him feel inferior, which wasn't the impression he wanted to give. He drew himself up to his full height and sucked in his tummy.

Raised beds stocked with roses, agapanthus, and lavender, brushed the men's legs as they ventured towards a large oak door that had been left open anticipating their arrival. Edward's enthusiasm to look inside the timber-framed house was all too evident. If Hammond hadn't felt so self-conscious, he would have been embarrassed by his colleague's display, but instead he followed with a false air of confidence until he was greeted by a heavy-set man in his fifties who grinned broadly at his visitors and stretched out a hand to welcome them.

"Good afternoon, gentlemen, I am Nigel Berwick. Pleased to meet you, please come in." His manner was friendly and jovial, nothing like the pompous squire attitude Hammond had expected. He shook the man's hand firmly and introduced Edwards, before they were led past the entrance vestibule into a large drawing room with a traditional beamed ceiling. Hammond settled himself into an armchair and refused a drink politely before plunging in.

"Mr Berwick, thank you for agreeing to see us. I promise you we won't take up too much of your time." He looked at the man directly, aware that there was a sense of familiarity about him but unsure where he had seen him before.

"I understand you wanted to speak to me about my employee Asli?"

Despite his welcoming air, it was evident Berwick was not a time-waster. This pleased Hammond. He ignored Edwards' gawping at the surroundings and took out his notebook as he spoke.

"Yes, as we explained on the phone earlier, we are very keen to understand why Asli was assaulted and to learn of the events leading up to the attack."

"It has been a shock. Why anyone would want to hurt such a sweet girl is beyond me."

"Do you know why she was in Dover that early in the morning?"

Berwick refused any bait that was dangling. "You haven't told me what time she was attacked yet, Inspector, but either way I would have to say I don't know. I hadn't seen her since the previous Friday. She had been granted seven days' holiday, and I am not one to question what she did with her private time."

"What are the terms of Asli's employment?"

"She is a carer for my mother who suffers the early stages of dementia. I have two self-contained flats within the gardens. Asli lives in one with my mother and provides 24-hour care for three weeks every month. She is granted one week's holiday per month."

"Does she have any other responsibilities other than acting as carer for your mother?"

"No." Berwick paused momentarily. "Well, Asli is a good-natured girl, and I do occasionally accept some favours from her if she offers."

Edwards' attention was now focused on the conversation. He raised an eyebrow at Hammond and attempted to hide a wry smile, but it was noticed by their host.

"Not sexual favours. I meant she may offer to help organise my files, or she will answer the phone and take messages, manage my diary on busy months, that kind of thing."

"I understand you own your own business?"

"Correct. My company offers industrial waste disposal services."

Hammond knew this already but affected the task of writing it down. "How many people do you employ?"

"I have 65 employees in total."

"Have any of your employees been granted a work visa to allow them to work for your company?"

Berwick snorted a reply and replied with a pointed finger at Hammond. "I see what you are trying to establish, Inspector. No, my employees are not all immigrants. I do not purposely advocate 'cheap labour', as many refer to foreign workers. Most of my staff are British born, although that is not a requirement of mine. I am not discriminate towards race, only a person's ability or willingness to work hard."

Edwards interjected. "Forgive me, sir, you do not discriminate between races, yet I recognise you from the BNP campaign posters from several years ago."

Berwick smiled, complimented by the recognition, whilst Hammond cursed himself for not researching their interviewee's history before blundering in.

"Contrary to common belief, The British National Party opposes the idea that any one race is superior to any other.

The party's ethic is to protect the cultural integrity of the British people by celebrating its exclusivity. I was an active member for several years and acted as a representative for the South East at one time, but I confess my loyalty towards the party was tested after the 2005 scandal."

Hammond raised his brow quizzically, encouraging Berwick to offer a hasty explanation.

"The London bombing in 2005 was a time when the nation should have pulled together. Unfortunately, the Party's publicity agents used it as an opportunity to suggest that had there been more supporters of the BNP policies, the event would never have happened. Hostility and blame were apportioned towards the non-British population in the country. I was, in truth, embarrassed by such a claim and attitude, so chose to discreetly withdraw my support."

"But you agreed with their policies in general?"

Berwick addressed Edwards, replying to the question directly. "Of course, I believed in their overall policies passionately, hence me wanting to act as the local representative. I am proud of my heritage. I did not want to see the country I love being integrated into the European Union; I want to see our nation be self-sufficient through farming and industry, without the excessive need to import goods from abroad. I simply want Britain to retain its British characteristics without the need to adopt foreign cultures as an act of hospitality for non-British residents."

Before Edwards asked another irrelevant question, Hammond quickly interjected. He had had enough of political debates during the last few days. He shot a look at Edwards, who succumbed by leaning back in his chair.

"Asli mentioned that you sometimes used her language skills as a translator?"

Berwick nodded. "Yes, on the rare occasions when I have had to discuss business abroad. She is a skilled linguist. But never officially and, like I said, it has only been very rarely."

"May I ask how you met Asli?"

"She was recommended to my brother, Kai, by a friend of his who knew I was looking for a care worker."

"Why did you not search via a nursing agency?"

"I placed an advertisement in the paper which attracted some nurses to the vacancy, but it isn't really medical care I was looking for. I really wanted a companion for my mother, so nursing credentials were not that important. I figured that Mum would eventually be moved to a care home if or when her condition worsened."

"Did you know Asli had been arrested and detained by Border Agencies for obtaining false identification and working in Britain without a permit?"

Berwick nodded. "Yes, she told me when I interviewed her for the job. To be honest, had I known before the interviewing stage, I would not have given her any consideration. But she was so gentle and honest, I was charmed by her. She is a wonderful companion to my mother."

"Do you know any of Asli's friends or contacts outside her employment with you?"

Hammond was answered by a shaken head. He quickly changed tack.

"Asli stated that she helps you by befriending people abroad who are seeking refuge here in Britain. She said she acts as translator, and has accompanied these people into Britain, sometimes covertly." He watched Berwick closely, looking for any reaction.

The man's tone was one of astonishment. "I don't know why you were told that. Maybe she was mistaken. I truly am mystified by such a claim."

"Do you own a boat or dinghy?"

Berwick was becoming flustered. "Yes, I own a Kelt 850 yacht. But I haven't used it recently because the cockpit fills with exhaust fumes. I've intended to get it looked at, but haven't got round to it."

"When was it last used?"

"Last summer I sailed across the Channel, and then Portsmouth for the weekend. I don't use it as much as I'd like."

"Does anyone else have access to it?"

"No. Well, I guess anyone could steal it, if they were determined enough. I keep the keys here at home, and there is a spare set kept with security where I moor it in Sandwich Marina."

"Are the keys locked away?"

"No." Berwick looked bewildered by the change of tone. Hammond had begun to interrogate rather than question.

"So, is it possible that the keys to your yacht could have been taken and replaced, or copies made without you knowing?"

"I guess so, but I really cannot see what you are inferring. What is it you suspect I may be guilty of exactly?"

Berwick looked at the detectives so earnestly that it almost swayed Hammond to believe in the man's claim of ignorance.

"Mr Berwick. Asli was attacked along with three other people. The others were not so lucky, so not only are we investigating the attempted murder of your employee but we are trying to find the killer of three more victims. Initial investigations suggest that all four victims, including Asli, had been detained against their will, starved, and systematically abused before they were brought into Dover illegally. We need to establish whether Asli was compliant in smuggling them into the country, and how and under whose instructions."

Berwick's eyes opened wide. "I absolutely have nothing to do with any of that!"

Hammond leaned forward slightly. "If, during our investigation, we discover that you have employed Asli for anything other than as a care worker for your mother, as you state, then we will want to question you further."

Berwick had regained enough composure to reply firmly as he stood up and ushered them out the room. "Well, in that case, Inspector, I do not expect to see you again, as I can assure you Asli was employed within the boundaries of the law."

He uttered the last words stiffly, but shook each officer's hand as they exited the house, and watched them retreat down the path to the car.

Their descent down the drive towards the gates was slow, but that did not prevent them from having to brake suddenly when a white van sped erratically towards them. The van's tyres slid on the gravel as it swerved to avoid hitting them.

Hammond stared at the offender with evident anger but the driver – a young male with a shaven head – stared persistently ahead of him, as if he hadn't noticed.

"Bloody idiot!"

They waited until the car had rejoined the main road before Hammond or Edwards spoke again.

"Berwick seemed genuine," Edwards said.

"I agree, but it is worth checking out his boat whilst we are heading back."

Edwards nodded whilst rummaging in his jacket pocket. He brought out a half-opened tube of Polo mints and offered them to Hammond, before taking three of the sweets and putting them all in his mouth. When he next spoke, the mints clinked against his teeth. "Lucky sod. I always wanted a sail boat. I used to go to the boat shows with my dad as a boy. "

"So, do you know anything about boats?"

"Only the basics."

"Good, it may help. What about Berwick's statement that the cockpit fills with the exhaust fumes? Would that be enough to make it inoperable for a while?"

"I don't know. At a guess, I would say all he'd need is an exhaust extender and a fitting for it to go through the hull, in order to fix it. I wouldn't imagine it would be a lengthy or expensive repair job. "

"But still possible to drive it?"

"I reckon the yacht would run, yes, but the pilot would probably feel pretty rough with headaches or dizziness because of the diesel fumes."

Hammond didn't answer. He just nodded and turned off at the junction heading towards Sandwich.

*

"Yep, I know Nigel. He's moored here for a few years now." The speaker had introduced himself moments before as Frank Sullivan, co-owner of Sandwich Marina.

"Are you aware of when Mr Berwick last used his boat?"

Edwards corrected Hammond. "Yacht. You mean yacht."

Hammond ignored Edward's correction and allowed his gaze to follow Sullivan as he walked across the office to a large filing cabinet in the corner. He waited patiently whilst the man leafed through papers.

"Yep, here we are. *Maisy's Dream* first moored here in 2011, June until September. Returned the following summer, and the next year, until we made an arrangement for Nigel to keep the yacht here as a permanent mooring."

'*Maisy's Dream* is the name of the boat... er, yacht?"

Sullivan looked up from the stack of papers that he had been referring to. "Yep."

Hammond leaned forward slightly, hoping that his change in body position would encourage Sullivan to be more detailed with his answers, but it was apparent the other man wasn't much of a speaker.

"Do you offer permanent mooring for other boat owners?"

"No, but Nigel is a good bloke."

"Why?"

"Why?" Sullivan looked the more confused out of the three men, although Hammond was beginning to feel he was in a sketch with the *Two Ronnies*.

"Why do you consider Nigel Berwick to be a 'good bloke'?"

"That's my business, isn't it? Why shouldn't I think he is a good bloke? Are you going to tell me otherwise, 'cos you should know I'll trust Nigel more than I'll trust any copper."

Hammond changed his tone. "I apologise, Mr Sullivan, it was no more than nosiness on my part. I do, however, need to question when Mr Berwick's boat, I mean yacht, was last taken out by Mr Berwick, or if anyone else had ever used *Maisy's Dream?*"

Sullivan scratched his chin stubble and contemplated Hammond before he answered.

"Me or my son Matthew usually accompanies Nigel out of the marina to pilot the yacht for him, because the tidal flows of the River Stour are tricky. It's best to only attempt it during the rising tide. Nigel gets nervous, because there is a danger of being swept into the low bridge when you approach. Exiting the river is equally difficult, because at high tide the marshes and beaches are covered. Many are tempted to head straight out to sea, but you've got to stay within a 35-metre lane that winds around the marshes. So yes, I will know when Nigel uses his yacht, and I can also state that no-one other than Matthew or myself have piloted it from here."

"I see, so as far as you know, when was *Maisy's Dream* last used?"

"About a month ago. I did a test drive following repairs."

Hammond raised his eyebrows. This update contradicted Berwick's statement.

"You repaired Mr Berwick's yacht? What work did you do?"

"New engine and replaced the pivot pin."

"Were you aware of exhaust fumes leaking into the cockpit?"

"Yep, all sorted when the engine was changed."

"So, the yacht is fully functional?" Hammond waited for the affirmative nod before continuing. 'And other than Mr Berwick, yourself, and your son, would anyone else be able to take *Maisy's Dream* out to sea without you being aware of it?"

"Possibly, although unlikely. The harbourmaster wouldn't miss it, though. He logs everything. Check with him."

*

Hammond and Edwards did as Sullivan advised and checked the logs with the harbourmaster, and all journeys with *Maisy's Dream* in and out of Sandwich Marina were accounted for. Despite the lack of progress made during that afternoon, Hammond had learned that Berwick was a respected man – so much so that Sullivan had become defensive when the man's character had been questioned.

It could be no more than Sullivan's affirmation of respect towards a fellow man, but to Hammond it suggested something more. Sullivan could simply have averted the question as to why he liked Berwick with a smile or a quick comment, but he had aggressively steered away from answering. Could it mean he was protecting Berwick in some way, or was he simply protecting himself? Had Berwick done Sullivan a favour of some significance? Possibly Berwick had given Sullivan a deal by disposing of any industrial waste on the cheap? Either way, Hammond decided as he turned off towards Folkestone, it was worth looking into.

*

"What do you mean, they've taken her?" Hammond stared at Dunn in astonishment.

"The hospital allowed Asli to be moved to another hospital. I don't know much more," she said uneasily.

"Do you know where?"

"No."

"So, what do you know?" Hammond's impatience was not directed at Dunn, although he knew he was sounding unreasonable.

She signed heavily, shifting her weight onto one hip and cocking her head with the slightest hint of attitude.

"Hammond, don't get agitated. It's not my fault. I was preparing the interview strategy as I was asked, but Morris told me there was no point as Asli was being moved and was no longer part of our investigation."

"Have you got Asli's file?"

"I handed them to Morris."

Hammond's hopes for reassurance from Acting Super-intendent Morris were thwarted.

"Border Force has taken over interrogating Asli. They were less than pleased to think that valuable time had been wasted, Hammond, and quite frankly, I agree that you were less productive than you should have been."

"I got the names and address of two of the victims, but I understood we had another day in which to interview Asli as a suspect."

"That changed the minute I read the notes you had compiled. It was embarrassing to see that an officer of your rank had wasted numerous valuable opportunities to retrieve intelligence from a witness and possible suspect."

Hammond sighed heavily with resignation. "So, what is going to happen now? I thought we were under instructions to keep this in-house for the time being?"

Morris nodded as he stood up from behind the desk and walked over to where Hammond stood. "That is still the intention. DCI Hunt will be in France later, processing the victim's addresses with the French Police. Any relevant information will be passed to us and we will continue the investigation. However, Hammond, you should know that if we weren't so limited with manpower, I would take you off the case entirely. So far, the media has been kept at bay as much as possible, but all that means is that we are under greater pressure to get a quick result."

"What about Asli? What will happen to her?"

"Officially, she has been moved to another hospital, She will be interviewed as a suspect and then, I don't know. If there is evidence of her breaching her terms of residence, I guess she will be deported, but it is unlikely we will be informed." Morris registered Hammond's look of consternation and patted his arm in an awkward but friendly manner. "If I can, I will make discreet enquiries and update you of any news."

CHAPTER ELEVEN

The invisible obstacles that Hammond had encountered during the investigation suddenly lifted on Wednesday afternoon, when Dunn introduced a possible eyewitness to the murders at Langdon Bay. A young woman had presented herself at the front desk, asking to speak to the detective in charge.

Her name was Sarah White. She had been away on holiday for the last week, hence she had not been aware of the public appeal for information. Whilst she hadn't seen the victims or their attack, she had seen a male who had acted suspiciously for a duration before the attacks, during her morning runs along the cliff. DCI Hunt postponed his visit to France and Hammond accompanied him in the interview.

"How would you describe the male?"

"Youngish. I guess, early twenties. Slim build. I think he had a shaven head."

"You think?"

"He was in a van driving out of the top car park at the time, so it was a difficult to tell."

"Would you be able to recognise him if you saw him again?"

Sarah nodded her head enthusiastically. "Definitely."

"What did he do to make you suspicious of him?"

"For several weeks, I ran past him during my morning jog. He would be huddled in a hooded sweatshirt, always in the same spot, looking out to sea. But he crouched rather than sat, and it was as if he was deliberately ignoring me or wanted me not to notice him. He never spoke or ever gave me acknowledgement, even though I passed him daily."

Sarah's brow creased as she thought back. "I can't really explain what he did as such, but he gave me the creeps. So much so that I got my boyfriend to run with me one morning. Jules agreed he was odd, so I deliberately changed my route after that so I wouldn't pass him any more."

"Did you see him at any other time?"

Sarah nodded. "On the morning the bodies were found at Langdon Bay. I ran earlier than normal, because Jules and I had to check in at Gatwick by 10am, which meant we had to leave home around seven. I didn't see the man during my run, but I noticed him leaving the car park. He was playing music really loud, which was drew my attention. I thought it was odd because it was early in the morning."

Hunt nodded. "So, what time did you see him?"

Sarah bit her lip whilst she thought back. "It must have been around six-ish, maybe a bit before. It was already warm and bright."

To their disappointment, Sarah was not able to remember the van's registration plate, but her information gave the team some hope of progress. Later, during the briefing, Hunt confirmed that Sarah's statement was a viable lead in the investigation.

"Her story checks out, and we have details that we can corroborate. We know that the sun rose at 05.32 that morning, so she would have been able to see the suspect quite clearly. The first low tide was at 02.25, and it was low when the bodies were discovered at six thirty. The tide started rising within the next hour, when we were there to process the scene. This means our suspect had a three-hour window in which to commit the murders and leave the scene."

"Cutting it a bit fine, though," Dunn interjected.

"I agree, but that could be simply arrogance on their part, or they may have expected the bodies to have been washed away by the tide before any visitors went to the area."

"Any leads on the van?" Edwards spoke up.

"From the description our witness gave, it could be a white Vauxhall Caddy. We don't have a registration, but it is a start."

The debriefing was short. The team had to proceed cautiously whilst the evidence was absent and facts were few.

*

"We don't yet have anything substantial," Hammond said to Dunn later when they were seated at the computers in the main office checking out the limited information already gathered. "We can't take it for granted that having two witnesses will lead us to the person responsible."

Dunn freed her hair from its ponytail band and shook it, seemingly relieved by the newly-acquired freedom. "Asli was there. She could identify the attacker and explain the events leading up to the murders. She could possibly give information behind the motive. In reality, all we really needed was her co-operation to get a conviction."

Hammond lifted his chin. "So, I've cocked it up?"

Dunn flashed a look of feigned surprise at his question. "No, well, maybe a little. But I can see what you were trying to achieve. Asli was in shock; she had survived a terrifying ordeal. We could have been accused of insensitive harassment, or it's possible her testimony may have been unreliable due to head trauma. At least, that is what her defence could say. But... well, we may have at least made an arrest by now."

Her attention was diverted momentarily whilst she studied her computer screen. "Hey, guess what? Your Frank Sullivan has a long record. Assault, antagonising a witness, selling illegal goods. Blimey!"

Hammond walked over to her screen and looked at it whilst she clicked on the options for more information. "What about his son, Matthew?"

A few taps on the keyboard later, Dunn shook her head. "Nothing. What now?"

"See if there are any links with Nigel Berwick." Hammond stood behind Dunn as the computer searched its database.

They were interrupted by Edwards appearing in the doorway to call, "Debriefing now!" They followed him quickly down the corridor, and gathered in the room where Morris was waiting.

"We have just received confirmation that Asli Rahim has identified her attacker as being the same man that Sarah White saw on the morning of the murders, which makes this man..." Hunt distributed copies of an e-fit to each member of the team as he spoke. "...our prime suspect. Kai Masters, younger brother of Nigel Berwick."

There was silence as the news was digested. Hammond felt the need to lick his lips, his mouth was dry. The face was familiar, but it was only when Hunt had voiced the connection with Berwick that Hammond remembered almost colliding with the driver of a white van the previous day.

"Asli Rahim has admitted working under the orders of Masters. He had secured her employment with his brother as a cover, blackmailing her with the threat of deportation if she did not comply. From her account, her official employer Nigel Berwick was not aware of this arrangement. We have only been given limited updates so far, but it appears that Asli Rahim has decided to co-operate, hence more information will be dribbling in as she is being interviewed. I want Masters arrested first thing in the morning. But in the meantime, we need as much information gathered about him as possible: where he went to school; contacts; anything else that can be used to connect him to this crime. From now on, we will focus this investigation entirely on him until he can prove he is not the guilty party."

For the first time since Hammond had met him, Hunt's smile looked genuine.

*

"You could have warned me!"

It was late in the evening, but Hammond's tiredness was temporarily abated by the opportunity to vent.

"Why?"

"The woman is arrogant, bombastic, loud..." He ran out of adjectives. "I can't see what Paul sees in her."

"But she makes him happy, that should be enough." As usual, Jenny provided a more objective viewpoint.

"Do you like her?" Jenny was not given the opportunity to answer the question before he continued. "Seriously, Jenny, she must be decades older than him..." The dismay in Hammond's voice made his tone change to a higher pitch as another thought crossed his mind.

"Do you think it's serious?"

"You mean, has Paul mentioned anything to me about his intention to marry Bettina?" Jenny was joking, or at least Hammond hoped she was simply trying to wind him up. The thought was unbearable. Paul married to Bettina? Oh God, no!

The sound of masticating gum on the other end of the phone was loud and incredibly irritating, but Hammond welcomed the opportunity to speak to Jenny. He didn't have many opportunities to talk leisurely on the phone, but there were occasions when he liked nothing more than to sprawl in the chair and chat about nonsense. Despite their quick exchange on the phone recently, he missed her. The unspoken rule was that they took it in turns to call – mainly to discuss his son – but Jenny had neglected to offer much detail lately, meaning Hammond felt out of the loop and craved information on how his son was faring. Especially since Paul was unlikely to disclose anything of interest to his father.

"I came your way the other day. I suppose I could have called in, but guessed you would be busy." The sound of chewing stopped momentarily as Hammond heard a loud slurp and subsequent gulping sound from the other end. He waited for Jenny to finish her drink before replying.

"I'm disappointed. It would have been good to see you. But I'm curious as to why you were here."

"I wanted to check in on Mary. I reckoned she would be lonely in that ghastly home they've moved her to."

The sentiment wasn't lost on Hammond. Her friendship with his elderly former neighbour had been a surprising one, yet it was undeniable. Jenny and Mary would have been inseparable had their age difference and their circumstances been any different. Jenny's friendship with him and Paul was testimony to the fact that she was capable of maintaining intimate relationships, yet it had taken Hammond a while to appreciate the girl. She was a complex individual. Immune to charm or small talk, she spoke directly, often lacking tact or diplomacy, and appeared to be disinterested in other people. Subsequently she was a mysterious character who had never disclosed information about any family or significant events in her life. The only clue of her history was when Hammond had witnessed Jenny communicating with his deaf neighbour Mary using sign language, although she had never offered any explanation as to how she had learnt it.

They discussed Mary's welfare, and Hammond promised to visit her more often, realizing to his shame that he had neglected to make contact with the woman for some time.

"Mary asked if you were settled and happy."

"What did you say?"

"That you were depressed, overworked, and sex-starved."

Hammond grinned despite her offensive tone. "Really? I wouldn't have said that."

"Oh yeah? So, you're saying I'm wrong?"

There was a pause as Hammond deliberated how to contradict her, then realised he couldn't and laughed. "Ok, I agree. I am depressed, overworked, and sex-starved!"

The sound of chewing had ceased and was replaced with the sucking of the e-cigarette. "It wouldn't hurt to try dating."

Hammond's grin stretched further. "Dating? Nah, I'm an old man now, set in my ways. I can't be bothered with trying to impress."

Jenny's answer was unexpected. "Oh, by the way, I told Paul that you are going to Lyn's wedding. He was really pleased."

Hammond's colourful reply was to an empty line. Jenny had ended the call.

The handset remained cradled in Hammond's palm whilst he digested Jenny's words. Despite his attempts to think of one, there wouldn't be a good enough excuse not to go to Lyn's wedding. In a way, it was a relief that Jenny had made the decision for him. Yet also maddening.

Maybe it wouldn't be so bad if he had someone to take with him, make it look as if he had moved on, even if he hadn't. *Is it that obvious I am lonely?* he wondered. It was true he felt too old to start dating again, but there was also the reluctance to invest in an intimate relationship only for it to be broken. Losing Lyn had been traumatic. He couldn't go through the heartache again. Yet he missed female company. He missed the fact that he wasn't seen as a man, as a desirable, rather than as a failed father or as a burnt-out detective. The handset was returned to its cradle as his bed beckoned from the other room.

CHAPTER TWELVE

Despite their preference for a surprise invasion on Elm Cottage, the team hadn't accounted for the electric gates. They opened after Hunt had identified himself, hence giving Kai Masters ample opportunity to leave via the back garden. Nigel Berwick met them at the turning area. His disheveled appearance and reddened face expressed his anger at their sudden early morning intrusion. He was still blustering with indignation when he was ordered to take them to Kai's annex.

A subsequent sweep of the apartment and grounds had confirmed Masters had escaped on foot. A patrol was sent to search the local area while Berwick was pressed for information as to where his brother may have gone, but it proved futile. The team had no choice but to return to the station to consider their next course of action. Hammond and Dunn stayed behind while Masters' apartment was searched thoroughly for any incriminating evidence.

"Same father, different mothers." Berwick said. He and Hammond were seated on the garden bench watching the forensic team arrive outside Kai's apartment.

"My parents divorced following my father's affair with Kai's mother. Kai was a result of that affair. I don't think love had anything to do with it. They never married, but my father allowed her to move into the house when she had Kai. It was a disaster right from the start, and she left when Kai was eleven. Being the older brother – we are 22 years apart, Inspector – I took on the responsibility of mentoring him." The last sentence was said ruefully.

Berwick looked into the cup he was holding as if searching for answers amongst the liquid contents. Not finding any, he looked up at Hammond.

"He was a handful growing up. Too much for my dad to take on, especially when he was diagnosed with bowel cancer. He died when Kai was 14."

"He found discipline difficult," Hammond said as fact. He had read the file on Kai Masters, who had had a long record as a delinquent. The first offences were mindless stealing from the corner shop, then it had progressed to burglary, and later assault.

Berwick nodded, his attention distracted as more officers exited Kai's apartment carrying sealed bags and loaded them into the forensics van. He stared at the activity for several minutes before turning back to Hammond.

"For the life of me, I don't understand this." Berwick looked so bewildered that Hammond was beginning to feel sorry for him.

"Were you aware of his influence over Asli?" Hammond questioned.

"No. I had no idea they even spoke that much. There was no need for them to. Asli lived in my mother's apartment. Occasionally, we shared a meal here at the house, and Kai was there some of the time, but no, not a clue. You say Kai was blackmailing Asli?" Berwick spoke with disbelief at the claim.

"The facts back up her story. However, there are several missing pieces to our investigation which is why we want to talk to him." *It was best to give Berwick hope*, thought Hammond. If there was a suggestion that Kai's involvement was down to a misunderstanding, the man may prove to be more co-operative.

"I wouldn't believe he was capable of killing anyone." Berwick sounded as if he was trying to convince himself.

"Kai has the opportunity to prove he is innocent of the murders, but we can't hear his side of the story if he doesn't talk to us." Hammond spoke casually but hoped his meaning was clear. If there was a chance Berwick knew where his brother was most likely to hide, now was the time to tell. But there was no reaction from the other man.

Hammond was alerted to Dunn waving to him from the entrance to the annex. He excused himself and joined her, noticing the evidence bag she was holding.

"Our possible murder weapon."

Dunn handed him the evidence bag and he studied the contents. It was a great find; particularly if the blank firing gun he was holding proved to be the one responsible for the fatal injuries. But despite the sense of jubilation at what was significant progress in the investigation, there was also the responsibility of breaking the news to Berwick. There was now even less doubt that his younger brother was capable of killing.

*

"A Beretta 9mm blank gun; a definite contender."

Edwards bent over the table where the gun was being exhibited to the team. He looked as if he was admiring the evidence bag contents.

Dunn peered over his shoulder. "What makes you so sure?" She spoke with a subtle overtone of sarcasm. Facts needed to be established before Edwards could offer an opinion, yet he was giving the impression he knew everything already.

The sarcasm was not noticed by Edwards, who had now picked up the object of interest and was studying the bag contents closely.

"Well, for a start, this is front firing. Most of the blank firing guns available in the UK are top or side venting to allow the ejected material to dissipate harmlessly, but the injuries on our victims suggest they took the full force of the pressure as the muzzle was held against them."

Hammond stood listening, He was often in awe of Edward's methodical knowledge, and this was another such occasion.

The man was studying the gun with concentration. He looked up at Hammond and stretched his back as he returned to his full height.

"If this is the weapon, then it tells us something vital about our suspect. Although this is a blank firing gun, it handles exactly as a real M85 would, and it would produce the same sound as a real live pistol. So, it is possible that the intention was to scare the victims with a warning shot or to apprehend them, intimidating his victims into submission by impersonating law enforcement personnel."

Hammond ignored Dunn's snort. She was evidently less impressed by Edward's display of knowledge, but he wanted to hear what Edwards was theorizing.

"It doesn't help us get an idea of a motive, though."

Edwards nodded and returned the evidence to the table. "True, unless of course Kai Masters simply gets a kick out of playing cops and robbers and it got out of hand."

Dunn interjected, "What about playing soldiers? There was a large amount of militaria collectibles amongst his processions. We've got boxes of the stuff here."

Hammond considered his colleagues quietly as he thought about his next course of action. Whilst DCI Hunt was in France retrieving intelligence on the named victims, Hammond was responsible for updating Acting Superintendent Morris with the team's findings. Until they could interview Masters, they had to present credible reasoning behind their every move; Hunt's orders had been to spend less time on possibilities, and so far there was nothing more than circumstantial evidence. Eventually he nodded.

"Nigel Berwick volunteered to come back with us. He is downstairs waiting to be interviewed informally. It is possible he may have some knowledge that could help us find his brother. In the meantime, we have Masters' mobile phone that had been left, so check his call log, see if there are any frequent callers or text messages that could lead us to his friends. Our priority is to find Masters, but we also need to look into any military connections that would corroborate that possible motive. I'll try to persuade forensics to move quickly on processing the items taken from Masters' flat. The more we have against him, the more justification we will have for his arrest."

*

Hammond didn't intend to keep Nigel Berwick waiting for as long as he did. He sympathised with the man whose love for his younger brother was evident, if not somewhat misplaced. But his stomach was threatening to eat itself, and the muffled gurgles coming from beneath his shirt wouldn't have sounded professional during the interview. The canteen was his first port of call, and a soggy cheese sandwich was retrieved from the fridge and eaten quickly before entering the interview room where Berwick had been waiting patiently for well over an hour.

Dunn arrived several minutes later, her hair having been re-styled into a chignon resting at the nape of her neck. Hammond noted her change of demeanor and watched as she pulled out a chair, having shaken Berwick's hand with a polite smile. Her manner was cool and efficient; nothing like the stroppy teenage attitude she had displayed minutes earlier.

Berwick was composed, but the furrow in his forehead made evident the concern he was trying to hide. He confirmed his relationship with Kai Masters for the benefit of the recording and leaned forward, resting his arms on the table before him, expectant for more questions.

Hammond produced a photograph of the blank firing gun and laid it on the table for Berwick's inspection.

"Do you recognise this pistol?"

Berwick coughed awkwardly and took time to answer. "Possibly. Kai has always liked replica guns. I knew he had one in his collection of memorabilia, but can't be sure this is it."

"What can you tell us about Kai's interest in the military?"

"Ever since he was a young boy, Kai loved anything to do with the army. He was enrolled as a cadet for a while when he was a teenager, but his lack of discipline got him in trouble. In one sense, he was the ideal soldier; he believed in the purpose of defending his Queen and country. But when it came down to interacting with the other boys, his lack of co-operation during exercises constantly got him into trouble."

"Can you name an example?"

Berwick looked as if he was about to answer, but just as he opened his mouth, he closed it again. He looked down at the table for several seconds before shrugging, then shook his head.

"No, nothing in particular."

"But it was enough to stop him joining the army?"

Again, Berwick paused before answering. "Yes. I helped him as much as I could, got references for him, even helped by employing a fitness instructor before his physical assessment, but he didn't get further than the interview. The rejection devastated him."

Hammond sensed restraint in Berwick's replies; He was tempted to push harder, but did not want to jeopardise further co-operation. He studied the man opposite him for several seconds, noting the tense shoulders, the quick movements of the hands when the man spoke. Berwick was hiding something, but he was there voluntarily; Hammond couldn't throw accusations without real reason. He arranged himself casually in the chair.

"Is there a reason why Kai has a different surname to you?"

"Well, my father and Kai's mother never married. She used her father's surname, which was Masters."

"Kai is a popular name in the United States, I believe? Is his mother American?"

Berwick looked surprised by the change in questioning, but Hammond's friendly expression seemed to reassure him. This was, after all, an informal meeting.

"Canadian. Well, her father was from Canada, but she had been raised single-handedly by her mother, who was Japanese. Kai is also a Japanese name."

"I see. Did you know her very well?"

"Kai's mother? No, I did not take any interest in her. She was the cause of my parents' divorce, so naturally I kept my distance. I was away studying at university when she got pregnant with Kai, and I rarely came home. When I did, we would be polite to one another, but there was no relationship to speak of."

"She left when Kai was eleven. Did she attempt to keep in contact with Kai?"

Berwick shook his head. "I have no idea. My father never spoke of her from the day she left, and neither did Kai. It was almost as if she had never existed."

"So, you do not know if Kai would try to find his mother?"

Berwick shook his head. "Unlikely."

"What about friends? Is there anyone, other than you, who Kai could run to?"

Again, Berwick shook his head.

Hammond drew the meeting to a close, thanking Nigel Berwick with a handshake and requesting an update if Kai made contact. He watched the man leave, trying to ignore the frustration building within him. He turned to Dunn. "Waste of bloody time."

She nodded. "Do you think it is worth tailing Berwick in case he leads us to his brother?"

Tempting though it was, Hammond wouldn't be able to justify the extra manpower. They already had Berwick's co-operation, and the last thing he needed was to be accused of harassment. He shook his head. "No, we still have some time. For now, we concentrate on what we do have."

*

The air in the main office was stale and humid. Wallace Hammond stifled a yawn as he searched the numbers printed from the call log. According to the list, Kai Masters had called a mobile number several times within a six-hour period on the day of the murders. Judging by the small number of contacts listed in the phone's inventory, it was evident Masters was not particularly sociable. Text messages would take longer to retrieve, but in the meantime, there was enough for the team to make progress.

A call to Sandwich Marina had lasted six minutes the day previous to the bodies being found at Langdon Bay. Following that call, several calls to a mobile number had been made, from ten o'clock in the evening until seven the following day. Each had lasted less than one minute, but were significant because they had been the only calls made that day, with no others made for several days previously or after.

Dunn returned the telephone handset to its cradle as she waited for Hammond to acknowledge her.

"I just spoke to the Candidate Support Manager at the Army Recruitment Centre. They remembered Kai, even though it was seven years ago, mainly because his behaviour during the first interview had been what they called 'disturbing'. They described his attitude as extreme patriotism. He openly shared his opposition to the inclusion of any soldier who was not what he termed 'pure British'. They held him responsible for antagonising another candidate who was dark skinned, and consequently he was literally licked out of the interview."

Hammond raised an eyebrow. "So, Masters' application wasn't even considered? Surely Berwick had known?"

Dunn looked thoughtful. "I'm not so sure that Berwick is as ignorant as he claims. He must have an inkling that his brother is unstable."

Hammond shrugged. "Who knows? We've met enough psychopaths in our career to have learnt that anyone with a mental imbalance can appear quite normal until something triggers their abnormalities. The question is, why now? If he had racist beliefs, could it have something to do with the fact that his mother left when he was so young? Maybe his mother returned to Japan. I haven't a clue what that kind of rejection would do to a young child, but it would make sense that the hurt and anger could manifest itself into a hatred of anyone or anything that reminds him of being abandoned."

"It's a bit far-fetched. Maybe he just has a screw loose," Edwards interrupted Hammond's theorising. "Our friend Frank Sullivan." He gestured to the print-out that Hammond was still holding. "It was his mobile number that Masters rang that day."

Hammond cast a resigned look at his colleagues. "So, who is the lucky boy or girl that is going to accompany me to Sandwich?"

CHAPTER THIRTEEN

Frank Sullivan entered the interview room. He was dressed in similar apparel to when Hammond had previously seen him, several days earlier. He stood inside the doorway and bit his lower lip when he recognised Hammond seated beside Edwards.

Hammond requested Sullivan to be seated which he did, following encouragement from the accompanying solicitor.

"I want to talk to you about Kai Masters." Hammond said.

"So you said earlier, but like I told you, I don't know where he is,." Sullivan replied, immediately defensive.

"I believe you, but I would like to talk about your relationship with Kai Masters. How long have you known each other?"

"A few years."

"Where did you meet?"

"At the marina. He was with his brother when they brought his yacht in one time."

"How long have you worked with Kai?"

Sullivan narrowed his eyes and shifted his weight in the chair.

"Who said I worked with him?"

Hammond ignored the question and waited, hoping Sullivan would incriminate himself. He didn't move for several minutes, confident that the enduring silence would become too uncomfortable for a guilty man. On this occasion, he was right.

Sullivan looked at his solicitor then back at Hammond. He seemed unsure. Edwards fed into his insecurity by leaning forward onto the table.

"Oh, come along, Mr Sullivan. Let's not play games. Was it drugs to begin with? It was easy enough to do, wasn't it? Smuggle a little into the boats you serviced then give a heads-up to those waiting at the destinations. You never told us Berwick sailed across the Channel last year. Went a bit wrong, though, didn't it?" Edwards sighed and shook his head. "You got a bit too greedy, stuffed too many illicit packets into the ventilation, and then unsuspecting Berwick nearly got gassed out by the fumes."

Sullivan wet his lips. "You've got no proof."

"It wouldn't be too difficult to find evidence, Mr Sullivan. Kai may be more eager to share details if it means he'll get a lesser sentence by implicating his accomplice. We had permission to look into your bank records. We have already had a quick glance at your accounts at the marina; you've received several large cash payments on a frequent basis. £12,000 was paid to you last week in cash. You didn't sell a boat, and from what we've seen in your work log, you haven't serviced a boat to warrant such a sum. Forensics can do marvellous things now. The minutest traces found in the boats you have moored and serviced would be enough. In fact, I wouldn't be surprised if they are lifting evidence now at the marina. I hope Matthew is being co-operative."

Sullivan shot forward in his chair. "Leave Matthew out of this! He has nothing to do with it."

The solicitor leaned to Sullivan and whispered, but the man brushed him away as if he were a fly.

"It wasn't anything big. It started with the occasional bag just for our own use, but then it became a good way to earn a little extra."

"By 'our', you are referring to yourself and Kai? So, when did it advance to smuggling people?"

"That wasn't my idea. In fact, I said I wasn't interested at first, but Kai said he knew a way that we could provide a service for desperate people; so desperate that they would pay any amount for help. He said that most trafficking gangs were being caught smuggling people in vehicles from France. The best way was to smuggle them in bulk across the Channel by boat. The English Border Patrol Cutter Boats were mainly looking out for makeshift rafts or dinghies, but a lot of the yachts moored at the marina sail around the English Coastline on frequent basis, so it wouldn't look out of place. Especially if we met the migrants halfway, once they got out of French waters, then collect them and bring them inshore."

"Are you saying that it was Kai Masters who thought of the plan?"

Sullivan nodded. "He suggested it to me. I wouldn't have thought it was possible, but he convinced me. Said he knew people who would invest in us. He said we would only have to do it a few times; that we could stop at any time."

"These people who could invest in your operation, did he give you names?"

Sullivan shook his head. He leaned back in his chair and crossed his arms, resting them across his stomach. "Look, I know I am no angel, but believe me, if it hadn't been for Kai, there's no way I would have done it. But it was so easy. I needed cash fast. If you've seen my accounts, then you will know I wasn't earning enough to keep the marina. And the marina, that's Matthew's inheritance. I wanted it for him."

"So how many times did you bring the migrants into Dover?"

Sullivan hesitated. "Once."

Hammond uttered a short laugh that resembled a cough. "Once? Why only the one time?"

"I did it the once and chickened out. I couldn't go through with it. I dumped the people where I was instructed and left sharpish. Truth be told, I've kept looking over my shoulder expecting to be arrested since."

Hammond studied Sullivan intently before he spoke. "Mr Sullivan, you have made it no secret that you dislike the police, yet you are being particularly co-operative. I find that odd. Could it be you are deflecting the blame onto Masters for what was actually your plan, but perhaps it went wrong? Maybe it was Masters who chickened out, not yourself?"

Sullivan shook his head. "No."

"Ok, let's say I believe you. When was the first and only time that you collected the migrants and brought them inshore?"

Sullivan paused whilst he appeared to think back. "Mid-June. There were three people waiting in a dinghy. I had a fishing boat that had been brought down from Plymouth awaiting collection by the new owners. I met them in that and brought them back."

"Where did you take these people?"

"On the beach just beyond Deal harbour. There is a golf club nearby where they could walk from the beach and be picked up."

"Who was going to pick them up?"

"Kai."

"Do you know where he was going to take them?"

Sullivan shook his head. He spread open his hands and looked at his solicitor, who was scribbling notes.

"And this was the first and last time you were involved?"

Sullivan nodded.

"Did you ever meet Asli, Nigel Berwick's employee?"

Sullivan's brow creased. "No."

"Did you talk to the passengers whom you met?"

"No."

"Did you exchange words with the dinghy driver you met halfway?"

"No."

"How were you paid?"

"In cash. An envelope was posted through the office door at night."

"On the 18th of August, a week ago in fact, Kai Masters rang you several times during the evening, then again throughout the early hours of the morning. Why?"

Sullivan licked his lips again. "He wanted me to go out again. Said it would be just one more time. He said that the original meeting place had been compromised, something had gone wrong and he needed me to go and pick them up."

"Did he say what went wrong?"

"No."

"Did you agree?"

"No. I didn't have a boat. I told him that. He was angry, said I should take his brother's, but I didn't. Truth was, I didn't want to be involved."

"Can you prove your whereabouts that morning?"

"Actually, I can. I got caught bonking the landlady of the Horse's Head pub." He smirked. "Her bloke has got the black eye to prove it!"

*

When Hammond arrived at the police station the following morning, a message was waiting from Acting Superintendent Morris asking to see him. It wasn't the best morning's welcome he could have wished for. Hammond felt hungover and exhausted. He selected a cup from the draining board and made himself a strong black instant coffee before heading towards Morris's office.

Morris was tapping on the computer keyboard when Hammond entered. The room smelt of freshly sprayed deodorant. Hammond licked his lower lip, tasting the chalky residue recently dispersed into the air.

"You asked to see me." Hammond stated the obvious.

"I wanted to congratulate you on the recent progress and am hoping you can assure me of an imminent arrest."

"Frank Sullivan is co-operating, but he maintains he doesn't know where Kai is."

Morris sighed. "Are you confident that his testimony is true?"

"We have nothing to suggest otherwise. I have doubts that the £12,000 he was paid last week was to keep quiet, as he maintains, but until we can talk to Kai I cannot prove he is lying."

"Did you check his alibi?"

Hammond nodded.

"I've been briefed by DCI Hunt," Morris went on. "The intelligence he has gathered in France corresponds to the account given by Asli Rahim. Interestingly, it also backs up Sullivan's account. Ten people were seen leaving Calais on the dinghy heading for the English Channel on the night of the 17th of August. Eight of those passengers were being trafficked into England to be sold for cheap labour. DCI Hunt has identified the place where they were held before they were taken onto the dinghy."

"Eight? We only found five, including Asli Rahim, and we don't know her involvement yet."

Morris was distracted by an update on the computer screen for a second before he returned his attention to Hammond.

"We know more now than we did. Asli stated that she was taken into France on previous occasions, where she met people wanting to pay to be brought into Britain. She was told she was needed to translate and counsel the refugees to enable their co-operation whilst being smuggled into Britain so they could start a new life. Each migrant paid whatever they could afford, with the assurance that they would be given safe and discreet entry into England, but also that they would have employment and permanent accommodation provided for them. They were offered housing in France until their deportation.

"Asli supplied the addresses where they had been given temporary accommodation by the organisers, as you know, but on the last occasion she was taken to where the people were being held, she was blindfolded and confined to the boot of a car, so she cannot tell us who took her there or how. For reasons DCI Hunt has as yet been unable to establish, Asli was kept with the migrants in a holding cell, without food and only one bottle of water to share between them. They were bound together to prevent them escaping, then were herded onto a boat heading for the English Channel. Subsequently, the boat was commandeered just before it left Calais. The driver was killed and thrown overboard. Asli wasn't definite about timing or location. She had been disorientated through dehydration, but was sure some of the passengers had been separated when they landed onshore. She and others were kept for hours near the beach before they were moved and attacked."

Hammond was astonished. "So, what happened to the remaining passengers? Were any more bodies found in the water?"

Morris shook his head. "No, the driver was found. No others."

Not waiting for an invitation, Hammond sat down in the opposite chair and took a long sip of coffee.

"So, let me summarise what I have understood so far. The migrants were paying to be brought into Britain believing they were to be given a new life, but instead were being trafficked?"

"Apparently so."

"Was Kai Masters the brain behind the operation?"

"Well, he was certainly involved, Sullivan's testimony supports that theory."

Hammond considered. "There was the mention of their operation having investors in the business, but no names of any investors were given. Sullivan said he hadn't been told and I am inclined to believe him." He paused before adding, "The boat was commandeered? Did DCI Hunt know why, how, or by whom?"

"It is possible that another organisation saw Kai's little operation happening on their turf and took back control. The profits in trafficking are huge; enough for one organisation to fight another for their business. Kai had to find an alternative plan quickly. It explains his panic and the phone calls to Sullivan that night."

"Can we be certain it was Kai who assaulted the victims found at Langdon Bay?"

"Hopefully, Forensics will confirm it was his gun that was used to inflict the fatal injuries. Asli has indicated as such, but she cannot be sure. Remember, she was severely dehydrated and confused at the time, possibly in shock as well."

Hammond forced a smile. "Well, Kai's anger at the change of plan explains the brutality. It could also explain the use of the blank firing gun; if it was used as a prop to encourage compliance, but then used as a weapon when his rage overwhelmed him." He sighed. "What about the other passengers? Are we waiting for bodies to be recovered in the Channel?"

"Apparently not. Asli stated that she believes they were taken off the boat first. They arrived on British soil together."

Hammond sat up straighter in the chair. "So, we're looking for more possible victims?"

"Wait. There's more." Morris paused. "One of the passengers was heavily pregnant."

Hammond was tempted to swear, but held back and gulped a mouthful of coffee instead. He expected Morris to speak but was surprised by the delayed silence. Morris surveyed Hammond for a prolonged moment before he spoke again.

"Before I asked you to meet with me, I spoke to DCI Hunt. He has an interesting proposition for you."

Hammond had an inexplicable urge to get up and leave the room. There was a sense he was not going to like what was about to be suggested, but he affected a casual air as he stared down at his cup.

"Do you remember Bradley Kelsey?"

Hammond stared back at Morris with an incredulous expression.

"Of course I bloody do!" The sharp response was justifiable; Brad Kelsey had been interrupted attempting to murder Hammond in 2011 when DC Michael Galvin had intervened and subsequently been killed. The image of Galvin's shattered skull flashed through Hammond's memory, causing the walls to appear as if they were closing in. Hammond swallowed and reminded himself to breathe.

"Of course. I apologise for appearing tactless, Wallace. That was insensitive of me."

"Yes, it was, but go on... what about him?" Hammond allowed his voice to resume its normal pitch.

Morris applied his weight onto both arms of his chair as he rearranged his position. It was before nine in the morning, but the heat was intensifying in the enclosed space, causing his shirt to cling to his back.

"There is a slight chance that Kelsey may be able to help us with the investigation DCI Hunt is supervising."

"How?" Hammond paused, deliberating how to continue. He felt that Morris was deliberately limiting the information he was willing to offer. It could be taken offensively; that Hammond couldn't be trusted to respect confidentiality of another ongoing investigation. Then Hammond realised that he had been guilty of doing the same thing himself several years ago. He had pursued a private investigation into a series of suspicious suicides at the request of a former colleague. His stubbornness to find the truth had become a nuisance to Brad Kelsey and his partner, whose trafficking operations risked being exposed. The investigation had been unofficial, hence there had been no back-up when it was needed.

Morris didn't reply. He merely continued to watch Hammond, whose frustration threatened to expose itself in another outburst. He waited silently until Morris resumed speaking.

"When Special Branch took over the trafficking enquiry in 2011 – using the intelligence you had gathered –, they were alerted to the possibility that a well respected member of the local community was involved in sponsoring the trafficking of girls used for prostitution. There were financial transactions connecting to Bradley Kelsey, but it was not enough evidence to link the two officially, although the suspicion was enough to justify discreetly monitoring their activities. There is a credible possibility that this company, having lost trade due to Kelsey's incarceration, looked elsewhere to continue the business and invested in the illegal migration business run by Kai Masters. I'll e-mail the full details to you, but short story is DCI Hunt wishes to pursue this line of enquiry."

"So, where do I come in?"

Morris leaned forward until his arms were resting on the desk. He looked uncomfortable; the heat was clearly getting to him. "It has been considered that you can get to Kelsey, get testimony that one of Kai Masters' suspected sponsors had paid to receive trafficked people with the intention of selling them on."

Hammond stared at the other man. The adrenaline that had now started pumping through his veins made him forget his earlier fatigue.

"Tell me how. Kelsey didn't give us anything when we interrogated him. Why would he suddenly co-operate now?" As an afterthought, Hammond added, "And why me?"

Morris smiled. "What is that quote about danger and love?" He clicked his fingers with his head turned to the side. "Oh, come on, Wallace, you like all that philosophy stuff..." Morris bit his upper lip with agitation and looked at him for help, but Hammond just shook his head mutely nonplussed.

"Ah! Got it! The man loves danger and sport. That is why he loves woman, the most dangerous of all sports."

Hammond, confused by the man's diversion, couldn't help himself by obliging, "What's Nietzsche got to do with it?"

"Love, Hammond. The greatest weapon of all. Kelsey's Achilles heel!"

Hammond was confused. He pushed his coffee cup further away from him as he leant on the desk. "Kelsey was infatuated with Patricia Goodchild, but she's dead."

Morris smiled. "Apparently not, Wallace. According to our friend DCI Hunt, Patricia Goodchild is very much alive."

Hammond's mouth felt dry. "Why me?"

"It's evident in the interview recordings that Kelsey had an extreme reaction to you personally. He hated you, yet there was a hint of respect. Whatever the reason, Kelsey is responsive to you; more so than to others. Offer him a bargain, an exchange of information. Offer him Goodchild in exchange for the name of the clients they served."

CHAPTER FOURTEEN

Wallace Hammond needed sex. At least, that is what his subconscious seemed to be suggesting, judging by the erotic dream he was startled awake from. The dog barking on the street below his open window had interrupted the moment when his seducer had begun to remove her bra. He hoped to fall back asleep and enjoy the fantasy, but he remembered the notes he needed to read before his meeting with DCI Hunt in the morning. He sat up in the armchair and rubbed his brow with the palm of his hand. The skin was sticky despite his shower a few hours earlier. The heat in the apartment was uncomfortable and unrelenting, and he craved the air conditioned office. But eventually he would need a bed, and an exhaustion-fuelled sleep would be better spent on a mattress than on an office chair.

He had printed the papers Morris had sent to his e-mail earlier without looking at them, but as he leafed through the pile of papers and saw Asli's printed statement amongst the intelligence previously gathered by DCI Hunt, his interest was re-awakened. He selected the pages with Asli's name in the header and began to read:

My name is Asli Rahim.

I wish to tell of the events leading up to my arrest on 21 August, 2013. This is a voluntary disclosure and I swear that this statement is true to the best of my knowledge, and that anything I fail to mention in this written testimony can be used against me in a court of law.

I have always feared men, I do not understand them. My experience is that they have only wanted one thing from a woman; a few more than from a girl, which is to hurt, ridicule, control, torture and then kill. My mother had warned me many times: stay away from them, they will charm you, they will appear to treasure you. and then they will hurt you in ways you cannot imagine. I had promised Mother I would heed the warnings. But I didn't truly understand what she had meant. How could men charm you when they were so dangerous? As a girl I had kept my promise. When men passed me in the street, I lowered my eyes. I remained quiet if any man addressed my mother, and I kept out of sight whenever visitors came to the house.

I never met my father but I knew about him. In Somalia, it is important to know your tribal ancestry. My mother taught me our tribal lineage 30 generations back, so that if the Militia came, I could identify my origins. My father had left before I had been born. At that time there were two tribes, Abgal and Habarrgidar, who were fighting; the two neighbouring villages were separated by a border. My mother lived in constant fear that the fighting would continue in her area of Mogadishu. My father had promised her he would take her to somewhere safe, she had believed him but then he had left her when she was pregnant with me. Through the grace of God, my mother had found work selling fruit at the local market. But we were poor. There was no money so I could not go to school. Sometimes Mother had to look for work elsewhere; she was gone for days at a time and then I would have to stay with neighbours. They did not treat me well. I experienced for the first time how a man can hurt a girl. I was eight years old.

It was soon after when Mother and I were walking home from the market, we saw an old truck driving towards us. The roof of the truck had been removed and a machine gun was poking out the back. Mother pushed me away from her suddenly, before the truck stopped; a woman got out the truck, put a gun to Mother's back, and forced her to walk away. Mother did not look back at me, to have done so would have endangered me also. From that moment on, I was alone. I could not go home; the village had been destroyed when the trucks came. To eat, I learnt how to beg. I slept where there was shelter; sometimes I would stay in camps or shacks, but I would have to move on when that area became violent.

I had no choice but to break my promise to Mother. I learnt how to befriend men. I met a black man, he was French. He wanted to know why I did not go to school, he promised to help me if I would become his special friend and accompany him to Europe.

I do not know how the French man had arranged documents for me. I never had any of my own, so I assumed he had said I was his daughter. Several months later (I cannot be sure how long we moved around; it may have been a year), we arrived in Paris. The French man took me to stay with a friend of his called Armand. I didn't like him, but I was given a mattress to sleep on and I no longer had to beg. I wanted to go to school. Armand said he wanted to help me, but he could not get papers for me. In Europe you have to have papers for everything.

I took care of Armand's place, I treated his visitors well, I learnt to cook meals for him and clean his clothes, I cleaned the apartment and he gave me food and clothes but never money. I tried to learn French, but it was very difficult. The French people did not like it when I tried to speak French to them. They are very proud of their language and it offends them when it is not spoken well.

When my body matured and I grew breasts, Armand didn't want me to stay with him any more; he said I was now too old to be his friend. For a long time I had to sleep rough on the streets of Paris. I slept in bus shelters, or in doorways. Sometimes I accepted liquor when it was offered. It kept me warm and numbed the pain when the men hurt me. Then I met an English man called Gareth. He liked me. He told me about English football and about London. It sounded beautiful. He told me that England is not like the Continent. I would need documents to get into the country, but he knew someone who could arrange to get me a Netherlands Identity Certificate and a plane ticket to Glasgow. From Scotland, I got a train ticket to London. I was directed to an agency who found me employment as an au-pair. I slept in a bed of my own, in a room where I had privacy. The children I cared for were well behaved and gentle and I grew to love them. I taught them to be proud of their country, they taught me to be happy again. The children loved me and didn't mind when I spoke their language badly. But then the family had to move away and I was left without work. I had to look for work at the job centre, but I could not give them a National Insurance Number because I did not have one. A few days later, I was arrested and charged with working in the United Kingdom illegally.

I was sent to prison for 12 months. It was difficult; the women in the prison didn't like me. They spat in my food, tried to provoke me with racist comments, and taunted me with words I didn't understand, but I stayed out of trouble. I obeyed the rules and refused to fight. In the mornings I studied English and Computer Studies, and in the afternoons I was allowed to work in the local community, clearing litter from the sides of the roads and sometimes factory work. A prison worker advised me that I should seek asylum.

SHOES ON A WIRE

I endured interview after interview, but eventually I was allowed to move to the Detention Centre. It was better than prison, but I couldn't work and my studies had to stop. I was not free; everything I did was monitored closely. At the Detention Centre, the officers talked to me as if I were stupid. I was given a lawyer to help me with my application for asylum, but I was not entitled to legal aid. A volunteer visitor came to help some of the detainees; the volunteer encouraged me to apply for bail for Immigration Detainees. They found me a lawyer, but I could not pay the legal fees, so I told them about my English friend, the man who loved football. His name was Gareth and I knew where he lived.

I calculated that I was 24 years of age when I was allowed to leave the court as a free woman. Gareth was waiting for me. I owed him for his help and was unsure how I would pay back the money that he had spent to help me. I did not want to serve men any more. Instead, I wanted to smell the sea, feel the breeze against my skin. Gareth said he knew a way, He knew people who lived in Kent, near the sea, and they had employment for me. He introduced me to Kai Masters whose brother needed someone to care for his mother. I agreed to go.

Hammond stopped reading. There was another page before the end of Asli's statement, but he had read enough. Morris had already briefed him on the details surrounding Asli's activities in France and on the day of the murders. He sighed heavily and contemplated the content of her statement. He did not doubt the veracity of her account, yet it was difficult to imagine the life she had described as being real. It never ceased to amaze him what cruelty some people endured at the hands of their fellow man.

When he became a police officer and saw how calculating and hateful some people could be, he had almost lost faith in mankind. But then Paul had been born, and his child had viewed the world around him with delight and awe. Despite what crises were being reported in the news at that time, what traumas had been happening in their emotional or private lives, his young son had continued to laugh and enjoy the wonders around him. And by doing so, he had taught Hammond to view the world however it suited him.

On this occasion, whilst Hammond did not despair entirely of the human condition, he was, in the words of Albert Camus, a fool for having hope. He had faith that Asli would be granted mercy at the immigration tribunal. There was no question that if she was found guilty of being complicit in people smuggling, she would be deported without the opportunity to appeal. The new powers about to be introduced in the government's flagship Immigration Act would allow Home Office officials to deport foreign convicts before they had the opportunity to make claims of malpractice under the Human Rights Act. It would be advantageous for the British nationals whose justice system would not be backlogged with cases being fought in court on behalf of foreign criminals hoping to delay their deportation. It would save the taxpayers time and money, but in the case of Asli, if she were to be convicted it would be a genuine breach of her human rights. Her testimony explaining her involvement in the crime committed by Kai Masters read more like a victim impact statement. If Asli Rahim was guilty of anything, Hammond considered, it would be naivety and misplaced trust, which made it all the more sickening.

He quickly became disheartened by the remaining papers beside him and decided they could wait for his scrutiny in the morning.

*

At 8.45am Hammond found DCI Xavier Hunt waiting for him in the station's reception.

"No-one on our team is likely to eavesdrop," Hammond said in response to Hunt's suggestion that they discuss their business at the coffee shop down the high street.

"Maybe not," said Hunt. "But the coffee there is much better."

The men sat in armchairs discreetly positioned in a corner by the window. It was early enough for the coffee house to be almost empty, with customers preferring to take away their drinks on their commute to their workplaces. It allowed Hammond to relax, knowing their conversation would not be overheard.

"My former superior officer would be horrified at the idea we're discussing police business in a public place." Hammond sipped his coffee and savoured the rich aroma, keeping the cup under his nose longer than was necessary.

"DCI Beech was a popular man. He has been mentioned to me several times since I arrived in Folkestone, and yet he retired two years ago!" Hunt stretched his legs from the armchair, causing the hem of his trousers to ride up the ankle, revealing a bright pink sock. "Why did he retire so early? Apparently, he had a few more miles left on the clock!"

Hammond shrugged. "He wanted to spend more time with his family."

Hunt sighed. "Yes, of course; a man with a family is a lucky man." He did not notice Hammond's look of surprise at the comment as his espresso was tossed to the back of his throat and downed in one swallow. Hunt replaced the cup on its saucer and gestured to the barista at the till for a repeat order. He waited for it to be brought to the table before he resumed their conversation.

"You have looked at the report I had sent to Superintendent Morris?"

Acting Superintendent Morris, Hammond reminded him telepathically before speaking aloud. "I read Asli Rahim's statement; the rest I have only managed to glance at."

Hunt offered an accepting nod. "Then you know we believe Asli's contact in England to be Gareth Carson." He did not wait for affirmation before continuing. "Gareth Carson has been the subject of discreet monitoring following his conviction in 2010 for attempting to defraud his company's creditors."

Hammond hadn't read that bit. He leant forward, hoping his surprise wasn't obvious.

"Gareth Carson is the eldest son of Robert Carson, a well respected former chemist who built up the pigment manufacturing company originally called *Carson and Sons* situated in Ashford. Following his father's death, he inherited the business with the role of managing director, until he led the company into near financial ruin through gambling debts. At the end of his reign, the company liabilities were just under £3million. When he knew the company was about to collapse, he attempted to transfer £1million of assets by backdating fake files. His directorship was banned following an investigation by the Insolvency Service."

"What stopped it going into liquidation?"

"The younger brother, Brett Carson; facts are a little murky, but the official story is that he managed to significantly decrease operating costs by selling a share of the site. He found a purchaser of the old assets, which amounted to nearly £1.2million, and continued to operate under the new name 'Carson Bros' with himself at the helm as managing director."

"What happened with the creditors?"

Hunt smiled, his expression suddenly enthused. "Good question! The creditors were appeased through monthly payments. At least..." Hunt paused for a second. "At least, that is the official explanation. However, there was no record of a voluntary arrangement proposal which, if it had been done correctly, there would have been. Secondly, every creditor was paid over 200 percent of their owed debt."

"That is suspicious?" It was a stupid question, but Hammond couldn't quite see the significance of Hunt's revelation. "Surely, if there had been an investigation by the

Insolvency Service, there would be the demand for transparency of the company's trading activities?"

"Indeed. But there were so many creditors that it was not easily monitored, and it was not the individual creditors who were under scrutiny. However, we now have glimpses of some of the transactions that occurred when Brett Carson took over as managing director. One example is the solicitor who dealt with some of the arrangements at the time when the company was taken over. The sum of £250,000 was placed in the solicitor's account for what was believed to be the anticipated settlement of some of the debts. There were subsequent bank transactions to several different accounts. Small amounts totalling no more than a few thousand to a few creditors, a larger amount to another. But again, it was only about £40,000 in total. Some more was then retained by the solicitor to pay for their services, and the remaining funds were then withdrawn, with that particular issue having been resolved." Hunt cocked his head towards Hammond with his eyebrows raised waiting for Hammond to take the bait, which he did, eventually.

"Money laundering?"

Hunt nodded and downed another espresso. Beginning to feel rather inadequate, Hammond took another sip of his own Americano. He was surprised Hunt wasn't trembling from a caffeine overload, but maybe the new-found enthusiasm in the other man was caffeine-induced. Hammond couldn't tell.

"So, where did the money come from originally?"

"It takes time, Hammond, a long time to find the original source! However, we have found potential sources, which is why we are now involved. Superintendent Morris explained to you about Brad Kelsey's suspected involvement?"

"No, *Acting* Superintendent Morris didn't really give me details."

"Or maybe you just simply did not read what he gave you?" Hunt did not wait for a reply. "No matter, your investigation in 2011 prompted an investigation into Mr

Kelsey's financial records when it was taken over by Special Branch. It was apparent that he always paid his bills in cash, including the purchase of a high performance, second-hand vehicle that he immediately sold to a private customer who paid by cheque, payable to Gareth Carson."

Hammond wanted to shake his head; his mind was reeling from confusion.

"So, what does that tell us exactly?"

Hunt threw his head backwards, allowing a laugh to bellow upwards to the ceiling. Hammond looked around embarrassed. The man was making him feel like an idiot.

"Well, at the very least it shows they are connected, that they are acquainted, and for some reason Kelsey had to pay Gareth Carson money. It is suspicious; such activity has no rational explanation, and none was given when Kelsey was asked."

Hammond was aware his forehead was heavily creased with concentration. He could feel the tension mounting across his brow and down his neck.

"So, the link between Gareth Carson and Bradley Kelsey is money from the proceeds of a sold car being paid from one to the other?"

"Now you are being pedantic! You know that Kelsey had clients whom he refused to identify; clients who paid for the trafficking of humans for prostitution, slave labour, and so on." Hunt waved the latter words away with the back of his hand. "Kelsey was convicted of two murders, as well as the charges of attempting to murder you, of course. Hence he is serving time now, but the other charges – including the other murders he was suspected of – couldn't stick due to lack of evidence."

Hunt leaned forward, ensuring Hammond's attention before continuing. "You are aware that there is no unified law against human trafficking in the statute books. Even if the trafficked people are identified, they are often unable to act as credible witnesses, usually because they are compelled to enact crimes whilst their traffickers enjoy impunity. Prosecuting the traffickers is difficult; often they are part of a criminal syndicate complicit in numerous criminal dealings, and trafficking is not a policing priority. But our murder investigation provides the perfect excuse to investigate both.

"Now a connection has been found between Bradley Kelsey and Gareth Carson, who was identified by Asli Rahim in assisting the illegal migration of foreign nationals seeking refuge; and there is a connection to Kai Masters, whom we know is involved in arranging their illicit deportation and then trafficking them. Lots of connections such as these make a long chain!"

Hammond sighed as he played for time, wondering what to say. His senses were confused by lack of sleep, the tempting aromas of almond croissants, and the urge to hit Hunt across the face for his arrogance.

"I agree there are connections, but they could be coincidence. It's certainly not enough to prove that Carson's suspected money laundering originates from the illegal trafficking or that he was connected to Kelsey and Patricia Goodchild's trafficking operation."

"Hammond, it is a cliché, but I will say it anyway; There is no such thing as coincidence in police work. If every parallelism is scrutinised thoroughly, it will be seen that it is nothing more than a myth."

Resigned, Hammond leant back in the chair. "So, what now?"

"We'll continue to search for Kai Masters. That remains our priority. Once we have him apprehended and forensics confirm his replica gun is our murder weapon, we have effectively done our job. We have witness statements placing him at the scene, we have a motive, and we have supporting evidence from Frank Sullivan."

Hammond interrupted, "Frank Sullivan is not a credible witness. He was trying to save his own skin. For that reason, it won't be difficult for the defence to trip him up under cross examination in court."

Hunt shrugged. "That is not my problem. What matters to me is that we have enough evidence to charge Masters and, whilst doing so, show that we are fulfilling our duties."

Hammond interrupted a second time. "I have to confess I am not satisfied that Kai Masters' suspected motive is credible." He almost blushed under the intensity of Hunt's responding stare.

"Explain." The other man's voice was clipped, annoyed, but Hammond ignored it and continued with his reasoning.

"Well, for a start, it is contradictory. On the one hand, we are supposing his motive is based on racist ideology; we know he opposed soldiers having less than pure British ancestry serving in the British Military, yet he was half caste himself. Secondly, if he did not want foreigners to enter the country, why enable their deportation into Britain? Then there is the means; why did he retain the murder weapon? Surely he knew that he had left traces of his DNA at the scene, so why not discard more incriminating evidence such as the weapon afterwards? Yes, the replica gun had value. It was, in his eyes, treasured memorabilia, but even if we discover that it is not the weapon which inflicted the fatal injuries, he could still be charged with the illegal possession of an imitation firearm."

Hunt considered Hammond's words momentarily. "Maybe the true motive was simply greed. True, there lacks certain logic, but it appears the murders were a crime of passion. It is unlikely that the killings were premeditated. When emotions are at play, mistakes are made, such as in this case. However, Hammond, it is to our advantage, so let's not over-analyse. Kai Masters is our one and only prime suspect. So, we find him and charge him."

Satisfied, Hunt stood up and extracted a £20 note from a soft leather wallet. "Please settle the bill for the extra drinks. I need to get back to the office, but you should take some time to digest what we have discussed. What we are asking of you is really very simple. Speak to Mr Kelsey. Extract all the information you can from him about Gareth Carson. Prove they are connected, and then not only will we be solving a multiple murder case, but we will be bringing down a trafficking organisation. That kind of success brings rewards, Hammond."

He turned to leave, then stopped. "Read the file thoroughly. I will arrange the prison visit for Kelsey as soon as possible, so prepare for that and I will organise more manpower to search for Masters."

Hammond stood up from the armchair. He pulled up his trousers from the waistband and then deliberately aimed for the pretty girl wearing a fitted t-shirt tight across the bust serving behind the till. She tipped the change into his cupped hand without glancing at him, already more interested in the next customer in the queue.

Such was life, thought Hammond as he exited the coffee shop. One minute you are at the head of the queue, the next you are pushed aside to make way for the next more viable contender. At that moment, his brain clicked into gear and he realised what he had missed all along; a fact so obvious and significant. The financial transactions were not the only connection between Masters and his possible accomplices. The profound thought was so sudden it caused him to miss the door before it swung into the face of a woman exiting behind him. Her exclamation was loud, causing other seated customers to look at him with obvious disdain. Embarrassed, he waved apologetically through the front window and headed hastily back to the office.

Chapter Fifteen

Wallace Hammond was like a dog with a bone; at least that was how DCI Hunt had referred to him the previous week. He wouldn't give up until he had every last piece of evidence that would confirm Kai Masters was responsible for the deaths on the beach at Langdon Bay. There were still too many unanswered questions for Hammond's liking. True, there was enough to warrant an arrest of their main suspect, but the rationale behind the arrest was still only circumstantial. An e-mailed report from Forensics confirmed that Kai Masters' replica gun had minute traces of scorched hair and tissue in the muzzle that corresponded to the victims' physiology. It was good news, but it was not what Hammond wanted to focus on at that time. Instead, he selected the internet search site and entered 'Carson Bros'. As soon as the results were displayed, Hammond bellowed such profane language at the screen that the entire office paused all activity for at least a minute.

The revelation that Hammond was eager to share was tossed aside within minutes as Edwards came bounding over to the desk. He registered the angry look on Hammond's face and hesitated for a second before plunging in with his news.

"You and I need to get to Oxford immediately."

Hammond's facial expression changed from anger to astonishment. "Oxford? Why?"

"Come on, I'll tell you in the car. Just get a move on!"

*

The air conditioning was blasting cool air directly in Hammond's face, which wouldn't have been a problem considering the heat and his agitated state, but the noise of the fan was irritating. He turned it off so he could hear Edwards clearly.

"The body of a woman was found in woodland. It is believed she is of Eastern European origin. She possibly died from natural causes, but foul play is suspected as it appears she was dumped by a third party just after or before death."

"What's it got to do with us?" Hammond automatically looked over his shoulder for oncoming traffic as Edwards joined the motorway. He was not a good passenger, and didn't enjoy not being in control of a moving vehicle.

"Oxfordshire Police thought it may be connected to our appeal for the mother of the newborn baby we found. Apparently, the woman they found had just given birth."

*

Two-and-a-half hours later, Hammond and Edwards were seated at the desk of Detective Sergeant Wendy Shepherd. She wasn't particularly tall, but she had an imposing air, possibly caused by her cropped black hair, the fringe cut close to the hairline and running immaculately straight across the breadth of her brow. Hammond was struggling with the urge to ruffle her hair and make her look less austere, but instead he set his features into one that suggested he was concentrating intently.

"The deceased was found at the side of a wide footpath near to the Nature Reserve here." A pen was used to point the area on a map placed before them on the table. "It is a popular area for walkers and there was no attempt to conceal the body, so whoever dumped her was confident she would be discovered quickly."

"An act of compassion or a careless manoeuvre aimed to make a quicker getaway?" Edwards referred to the photos DS Shepherd was in the process of handing to them.

"We don't yet know whether she was still alive when she was left there. She was emaciated and filthy, which suggests she hadn't been in a comfortable environment for some time. Preliminary examination of the body suggested that she had died from postpartum haemorrhage. There was blood around the body at the scene, but that does not rule out that she hadn't died beforehand and fresher blood pools had spilled as she was dumped."

The photographs showed the back of a very thin woman. Her dress – soaked dark with blood – clung to her legs, which looked tangled together in the soiled fabric. Her face was pressed against dirt, but it was evident they were looking at a young woman no older than her mid-twenties.

"Any residual soil in the nostrils or mouth?"

"Nothing that suggests she was breathing. Obviously, we will know more when she is opened up, but it is unlikely anything will be found in the lungs or airways. With this amount of blood loss, she would have been barely conscious; any breathing would have been particularly shallow. I am postulating of course but..." Detective Sergeant Shepherd gestured to the pictures to explain her reasoning.

"So, you believe she may be our missing mother?" Hammond nodded as he spoke. It was credible. A simple blood test would tell them for sure. The thought of re-uniting mother and child quickened his breath, almost as if he hadn't breathed fully until that moment.

"There is a strong possibility. There have been no reports of a newborn child being found near the area and she had given birth recently. So it is either your missing mother, or a child has been abducted by a third party. Either way, we need to check all avenues of enquiry."

"So, our third party. Any clues as to how many people are involved, or their intent? Anything at all?"

"We have the area currently being examined by a forensic team, but I would like you to come with me to the site, have a look around and see for yourselves. You can use the time whilst the samples are being gathered."

*

It was not the first time Hammond had witnessed how quickly a countryside scene with its rural natural beauty and tranquility had been spoiled the moment a human corpse had been discovered. The scene would have been idyllic had there not been police tape strung up between trees and several people dressed head to toe in blue paper suits tiptoeing through fern and wild garlic.

DS Shepherd navigated their way towards an area that had been cordoned off.

"This is the spot where the body was discovered about four hours ago by a cyclist, from whom we have taken a statement. You can read that later, if you like. Paramedics were called, then the coroner and our response officers, so there have been several possible contaminants to the area."

Hammond was studying the ground approaching the area. They were standing near a wide track that ribboned its way through dense woodland. Despite its natural setting, the route was well maintained, the path smooth and wide enough to enable access for wheelchairs, cyclists, and foresters.

"These tracks here. I presume that was the ambulance?" Hammond was crouched down examining several tyre prints moulded in the soil. He stood up. "There are only three sets of footprints here. The deceased was wearing slip-on shoes with a worn tread, but there should be some footprints other than the paramedics and first responders. Without being intentionally patronising, I assume you have taken note of the cyclist's clothing?" He registered DS Shepherd's nod of confirmation. "So, we know that the deceased did not walk here. The other set of tyre tracks suggest she was driven here and, since there are no other footprints, that can't be accounted for. We can assume she was pushed out of a vehicle. Likely to be a van."

Detective Sergeant Shepherd frowned as if contemplating his reasoning before asking, "Why a van, not a car?"

Hammond pointed to the tracks that ran horizontally across the track. "These tracks do not run parallel to the track. The vehicle approached from the entrance. Stopped and then manoeuvered so that the back of the vehicle was pointing to the side of the footpath. There are no footprints, so it is likely that the body was pushed out and dropped onto the ground, hence her position. If the perpetrators had driven her in a car, it would not be so easy to have rolled her out, even by pushing from the other side. It would have required getting out of one side of the car, walking around, and then pulling the body out onto the ground. There would have been more disturbances in the soil and footprints."

Edwards agreed with Hammond's logic. "How long will it take before we can match the tyre mouldings?"

The scoff that emitted from DS Shepherd was not intended to be discreet.

"I don't need to tell you about the backlog of evidence awaiting processing. How long is a piece of string? The priority will be in trying to identify the deceased and establish cause of death. If there is seen to be foul play, we will continue the investigation, but I can't guarantee that you won't be handed the responsibility of the investigation if she is confirmed as the mother of your abandoned infant."

Edwards glanced at Hammond, who now stood in silence with his hands in his trousers pockets, his shoulders slouched, and head bowed as in deep thought.

Edwards answered, "If she is, we know she had travelled from Kent. We just need to find out where she came from and why her baby ended up at the side of the road."

DI Shepherd indicated they should exit the area. As they headed back to the car that waited to take them back to the station, Hammond spoke.

"If she is our missing mother, I suspect she was brought covertly into the country from France by a small vessel, along with eight others. Four were killed, one was almost killed, and three more were taken to a meeting place by Kai Masters and handed over to their next handler."

Edwards turned in surprise as he opened the car door. "You can't possibly make such assumptions!"

"Yes, I can. Better still, I reckon the van that brought her here was a white Vauxhall Combo 1700 Twinport, reported stolen from a vehicle hire firm. Don't frown, Edwards, it's a lead and one I am confident will bring results."

*

The return drive started in silence before it became uncomfortable. It was not that Edwards or Hammond had nothing to say, more that they were pre-occupied with their own thoughts. Hammond understood Edwards was keen to return home quickly to appease his wife. It wouldn't be the first time that family discord evolved around late homecomings, and Edwards was a dedicated family man. Every missed bedtime story to his children was a grievance to him, but in Hammond's experience, police work was uncompromising.

The radio was turned loud as they exited the roundabout and headed towards the M40, but after several hits from the eighties, the repetition of local radio adverts became irritating, as did the small talk between radio hosts. The radio was turned off in the middle of a discussion about the size of Beyonce's posterior. It meant little to Hammond, who did not know who Beyonce was, although the subject matter was enough to break Edwards' silence as he commented her backside had indeed gotten a lot smaller than in previous years.

The passing landscape did not vary enough to provide distraction from the monotony of the journey, although as they passed several pubs, Hammond began to wonder when he had last visited one. It seemed an age since he had last played darts or sat amongst a group of relative strangers discussing news topics, walking with a stoop to the toilets to avoid the irregular sloping ceilings, then bashing his head on a beam he hadn't noticed until it was too late.

Now lost in his reverie, his mouth watered at the thought of a filled pint glass with a frothy head floating upon liquid golden nectar, droplets of condensation slowly gliding down the glass, forming a ring on a solid wood bar littered with potato crisp debris. He slowly became aware of Edwards talking to him and, with some reluctance, pulled himself out of his daydream.

"I said," Edwards repeated, "what are you going to tell DCI Hunt?"

Hammond shrugged. "I will tell him what we know."

Edwards faced Hammond momentarily before returning his attention to the road ahead. "What we know, or what you think you know?"

Hammond wasn't offended despite the implication that there was nothing other than hypothetical theories.

"Maybe a bit of both. I will decide as I am talking to him. Either way, this investigation won't be closed simply by arresting Masters when we find him. Especially now there is another connection..." He emphasised the point further. "A *credible* connection between our victims, Kai Masters, and David Hargreaves, the employee from Carson Bros." He noted Edwards' frown and turned his body sideways in the passenger seat to face his colleague directly.

"Asli Rahim was helped by Gareth Carsons from Carson Bros to find employment. It can't be a coincidence that she was referred to Nigel Berwick through Kai Masters, who intended to bring migrants illegally into the country. So, we know that Gareth Carsons and Kai Masters are acquainted. The fact that she wasn't offered employment within the Carson Bros factory suggests his motive wasn't charity. Furthermore, we also know that the managing director of Carson Bros, where David Hargreaves was employed, and Kai Masters were involved in incidents within days of each other. Kai was witnessed driving away from Langdon Cliffs, and forensic analysis has confirmed he was present at the murder scene. Two days earlier and only several miles away, Brett Carson was involved in a road traffic accident which involved the fatality of a newborn baby that we now suspect was born to a mother whose body was found just over a hundred miles further north."

Edwards shot a look sideways at Hammond.

"No. David Hargreaves was the guy who saw the baby thrown from the back of a vehicle."

Hammond smirked. "Yes, that is what we were told. That is what we were made to believe."

"But you interviewed David Hargreaves yourself!"

"No. I interviewed the man who *presented* himself as David Hargreaves. I didn't check his identity because I had no reason to. What I now realise was that Brett Carson expected us to turn up, so probably asked the receptionist to inform him when we arrived, with the excuse that David Hargreaves would not be available. When DCI Hunt identified Gareth Carson as the man responsible for introducing Asli Rahim to Kai Masters, I recognised the company name so I searched Carson Bros on the internet. Brett Carson's image popped up and I recognised him as the man I had been led to believe was David Hargreaves, so checked further. David Hargreaves had been in Paris that week for a business meeting."

Edwards held up a hand to pause Hammond's narrative. "Hang on, I'm confused. David Hargreaves had the accident, or didn't he?"

"No. Brett Carson was driving behind the white van. It was he who reported the infant being thrown from the van, but he used the identity of David Hargreaves, knowing it was likely we would check Hargreaves' background as a precautionary measure."

"But surely the response officers checked his driving licence when they attended the scene?"

"Not necessarily. Carson appeared to be a man in shock. Chances are, after they took the precautionary alcohol breath test, the officers were distracted by the paramedics and the activity at the scene."

Edwards swore quietly under his breath. He was silent for a moment before he added, "Devious sod. So, there is a chance that the Carson brothers are involved in the operation run by Kai Masters. I get it. What I don't understand is why Carson risked drawing attention to himself by phoning the police in the first place. He could have continued without reporting the infant's death and let it be found later."

"A speed camera picked up the Vauxhall Combo Van earlier. It would have shown Brett Carson driving behind, and there would have been a chance, however slight, that any further investigation would have exposed their reason for travelling together—"

"Which was?" Edwards interrupted.

"Overseeing the handover of the people delivered by Kai Masters."

Edwards nodded slowly. "So, by providing an explanation early on, he would likely be discounted from any further enquiries. Smart move. Although..." Edwards wagged a finger over the steering wheel. "He is an idiot for not thinking he would be recognised eventually."

"Possibly, but that may be simply down to his own arrogance."

Edwards' smile disappeared as he considered Hammond's reasoning. Then he shook his head. "No. It doesn't fit. The baby was killed two days before the bodies were found on the beach. If the mother and baby had been brought into England by Kai Masters and then handed over to Brett Carson, it would have been on the same day."

Hammond mused for moment. "Unless the others were incarcerated when they arrived, and then killed by Masters two days later."

Edwards shook his head. "Unlikely. Why would he do that? And where would he hold them?"

"We know from Sullivan's account that Kai was panicked; evidently something had gone wrong. If he had commandeered a boat used in another people smuggling operation, then he would have had to act impulsively and make sure he would be able to hand the passengers over as quickly as possible. Brett Carson arranged to take three people – likely to have been the fittest or the most profitable. Sullivan's testimony suggests it had been an unplanned operation, hence Masters may have had trouble finding another buyer immediately. The old bunkers or the disused tunnels would have made good hiding places whilst he waited. In the meantime, the victims are suffering from starvation and dehydration. They cannot walk to the nearest car park, which is a distance away. To him, it was just collateral damage. When goods spoil, they are discarded."

"The manner of their deaths suggests he wasn't so rational."

"He was probably infuriated by the way it had all gone so wrong. You said yourself, the gun may have been used as a prop. It wasn't intended to be used as a weapon".

"It's just theorizing. That's not enough to connect the two incidents."

Hammond had an idea. "Asli Rahim's statement said that she thought they had been kept for hours after they had been taken off the boat. Some of the passengers had been separated whilst she and the others were left there. That could be enough."

Edwards didn't say anything, but simply inclined his head as he thought about it. He didn't look convinced. "What made you consider the two cases were connected?"

Hammond paused as he realised he hadn't spoken of his earlier meetings with DCI Hunt. Quickly, he skimmed over the information given to him: about Hunt's association with Europol and their trafficking investigation; about the Carson Brothers; how they had come under the radar years previously for suspected money laundering; and lastly, their possible association with Bradley Kelsey and Patricia Goodchild's trafficking operation.

"Wha..!"

The car braked suddenly, causing cars behind them to honk their displeasure at the sudden move. Edwards apologised by waving a hand to them in his rear-view mirror.

"Bradley Kelsey? As in *the* Brad Kelsey?!"

Hammond pulled his lips tight across his mouth with disdain at the subject matter.

"Yes. Apparently, our investigation from years previously highlighted Carson's murky financial dealings. Long story, which I'll explain later, but to keep it short, Acting Superintendent Morris wants me to see Kelsey and squeeze information from him."

Edwards had become fidgety since the mention of Kelsey. He hadn't forgotten the events leading to Detective Constable Michael Galvin's death, either. It was a subject that had inadvertently intertwined their and Lois Dunn's lives permanently. They had all witnessed an event so tragic that it would forever stain their memories in a way that time could not erase.

There was silence for almost an hour. Hammond watched his colleague intermittently, wondering what Edwards was thinking. Eventually the man spoke.

"So, we need to get the team together for strategy planning. What's the priority?"

Hammond noted with relief they were now heading closer to Maidstone. Soon he would be back in his dingy apartment with his feet up. He tried to remember whether there was any chicken curry left in the freezer. He hoped so.

"Ideally, we want all our victims identified, but that seems impossible since they were found without any identification or personal belongings. That leaves Kai Masters as our priority; we continue to search for him. There is now the possibility that he has been given shelter by the Carson Brothers, so we need to get them in just as quickly. The rest will be decided by

DCI Hunt. I need to see Brad Kelsey, so it is possible that you and Dunn will be interviewing them."

Edwards manoeuvered onto the motorway's third lane to overtake a lorry. As they passed, Hammond looked up at the driver's cab and for an inexplicable moment thought he saw his own father who had been dead for years. He blinked and looked again. The driver looked nothing like his father. *I am going mad*, he thought.

"DCI Hunt wants arrests, and quickly. All we have so far is Frank Sullivan's admission to drug smuggling and a possible charge of incitement, if the CPS decide we can proceed. The more people brought in and charged, the better DCI Hunt's record looks, which, to be honest, is all he cares about. Every stone must be unturned with discretion, so we don't step on the toes on Europol's investigation. Personally, I want to bring the whole trafficking operation down, but that is not my job. So, I will do the best I can to expose as many of those involved."

Edwards offered an insincere smile. "We may get lucky," he said, sounding less than optimistic.

Chapter Sixteen

Less than half an hour after bidding Edwards a good evening as they left the station, Hammond parked his car, relieved to have found a parking space only a minute's walk from his apartment. It was a rare find, and one that gave him a sense of optimism. He was hungry, so the sooner he could find the frozen chicken curry he had been anticipating, the better. His footsteps quickened at the thought, and his hand flicked through the several keys on his keyring until he grasped the front door key and aimed it forward. His steps faltered as he neared the steps leading to the apartment entrance.

Jenny was leaning uncomfortably against the neighbouring wall. Her posture was awkward; one leg was crossed in front of the other at the ankles, displaying her canvas training shoes with their fluorescent laces to full effect. Large cardboard pizza boxes were clasped against her chest. Her hair had grown since he had last seen her, and he noted to himself that longer hair suited her.

She looked up as he approached, and peeled her backside from the wall, grimacing a little as her legs took her full weight.

"Stiff," she said to him as a word of explanation.

"Been here long?" he asked, although it was evident she had been waiting a while.

Jenny nodded and shook the pizza boxes to attract his attention towards them. "I brought pizza," she said, stating the obvious.

It wasn't the meal Hammond had wanted. Pizza was, in his opinion, food for the less sophisticated diner, but his hunger accepted the offering Jenny had provided. It had gotten cold, but congealed cheese was just as good.

He nodded his appreciation to Jenny as she joined him at the kitchen table with a large bottle of tomato ketchup that she proceeded to squirt inside the box. She ignored Hammond's look of distaste at the action, and tore off a slice of ham and pineapple before shoving it in her mouth and speaking at the same time.

"This is a short visit. I'm not staying."

"Fair enough. But it's always good to see you, you know that."

"Don't lie. The last thing you wanted was an unexpected visitor coming round." Jenny got up from the table and ventured to the fridge. She glanced inside and immediately looked disappointed. She nudged the fridge door closed with her shoulder, then proceeded to fill a glass with tap water before seating herself back at the table.

"With anyone else. But you and Paul are always welcome."

"So, Bettina isn't welcome here then, even if she is your future daughter-in-law?"

Hammond choked on a mouthful of margherita. He was suddenly agitated. "Oh no. The woman will not be my future daughter-in-law, not if I can help it."

Jenny's hand holding the second slice of pizza paused mid-air as she studied him for a few seconds, then she said, "If Paul makes the decision to marry her, it won't matter what you think. He'll do it anyway."

Hammond stopped chewing. "Are you trying to tell me something?" He registered hesitation on her face and leaned forward on the table. "Jenny, don't muck me around, Is Paul seriously intending to marry that woman?"

"Maybe."

"Jenny! Tell me!"

Jenny looked directly at him across the table, her chin jutted forward a little, hinting defiance.

"Paul mentioned they had discussed the possibility. That's all I know, but I figured you should get used to the idea before they make plans."

Hammond had lost his appetite. He sat with his bowed head cupped in one hand, the other lay on the table beside his abandoned pizza.

"Jenny, I can't let him. Seriously, why would he want to marry her? I am sure she has her merits, but she's arrogant, opinionated, bombastic, cumbersome..." He ran out of adjectives, so added, "...not to mention she's old enough to be his mother!"

Jenny laid a reassuring hand on his arm for a second before moving it away self-consciously. It was rare for her to be so tactile, and the meaning wasn't lost on him.

"Wally, your son is in love. Bettina makes him happy. That should be enough."

True to her word, Jenny didn't stay long. She left him with the congealed remains of the pizzas and a reminder to contact Paul. 'He needs his father,' she had said.

Hammond watched Jenny leave, and considered the reason for her visit. *My son is lucky to have such a good friend*, he thought. Then he corrected himself. *We both are.* He retrieved his mobile phone from his trouser pocket and started to write a text message to Paul, but then discarded it and decided he would phone his son the next day.

*

Detective Sergeant Lois Dunn had been busy. The e-fits of the victims found at Langdon Bay had been re-issued to various media outlets, hoping to identify them. She had less faith that the appeal for information would provide any leads, but she had persisted nonetheless. At the same time, she had attempted to track down any contacts of Kai Masters that they had not yet considered. Her tasks were necessary but proving futile. Her demeanor was one of despondency and frustration, which was why she inwardly groaned when she saw Wallace Hammond heading towards her.

The sweat stain appearing under Hammond's shirt sleeves was becoming embarrassing, but nothing could be done to hide it, so he affected a casual air as he proceeded through to the main office. He saw Dunn and purposely beamed what he hoped was a charming smile.

"I owe you an apology," he said.

Dunn gazed at him with a neutral expression but didn't say anything, which wasn't what he had predicted. Her silence and lack of surprise made him uncomfortable, and for a moment he wondered how many things he needed to apologise for.

"You were right to be suspicious of David Hargreaves."

He noted a twitch at the side of her mouth. It was subtle but encouraging. He quickly updated her with his recent findings. She listened, occasionally asking him to elaborate details, but slapped his arm when he finished, praising his progress.

"Good work, Sherlock! I guess the meeting I was heading to is to plan the interviews?"

He shrugged, encouraged by her response. "Yes and no." He explained what DCI Hunt had unearthed regarding Gareth Carson, but hesitated when he saw her stiffen at the mention of Bradley Kelsey.

"It's just to establish whether the Carson Brothers have a vested interest in the trafficking operation run by Kai Masters. That's all."

Her expression was unreadable. She paused for a minute before answering. "But why you? We knew there were clients of Bradley Kelsey that would remain undisclosed. The fact that the Carson Brothers may be one of them doesn't change the fact that there are more. Just exposing one or two won't be enough to shut down trafficking crime. You're not even qualified for that kind of investigation, anyway!"

Her outburst revealed a hint of resentment. He understood the hurt and anger that was stirred by the mention of Kelsey, but her words were precise and directed at him personally.

"What's that supposed to mean?" he asked incredulously.

"Wallace, you are a Detective Inspector. The operation run by Patricia Goodchild and Bradley Kelsey had been taken over years ago. The investigation into their involvement with human trafficking has probably been going on under our noses ever since we arrested Kelsey. It's huge; more than you or I could deal with. You have no ambition to climb the ranks, you aren't interested in brown-nosing or gathering Brownie points, but yet you get the recognition for being a good detective, you get the work that outranks you, and no-one questions it. Yet me..." She stabbed a finger at her chest. "Here's me wanting to achieve, desperate to be recognised, to be promoted. I am the one with the instincts, the drive, the relentless ambition to be something in the police force other than your right hand!"

It was as if her words were knocking him over, and Hammond leant against the wall as he hesitated, wondering how to answer. He noted her tired eyes brimming with disappointment and envy.

Eventually, he spoke. "I think you are missing the point, Lois. I have been asked to speak to Bradley Kelsey simply because the man hates me so much that I am more likely to unsettle him. That's all it is. There is no credit being handed to me for having the skills attributed to a higher rank. Far from it. Truth is, I think I am being made a scapegoat." He lowered his voice. "There is no chance that we will retrieve any information from him. If the Carson brothers did buy trafficked people from him and sold them on, it was years ago, so it is very unlikely we can prove it. I doubt even he knows the identity of their clients. Patricia Goodchild is the only one with that information, and she's pretending to be dead somewhere." He paused when Dunn's eyebrows shot up in surprise.

"That is all I know, but somehow I have to convince the man that he should tell me everything in exchange for information I don't have on her whereabouts."

Lois Dunn's mouth formed an "Oh" expression.

"Exactly. I am doomed to fail. But then the blame will be on my incompetence rather than the failings of Special Branch's investigation. Think about it; it would be less messy to 'encourage' me into early retirement if I fail to deliver the information they want rather than face an internal enquiry later."

Dunn looked at him with a softened expression. "I'm sorry," she said.

*

They walked together to the meeting room, where they spent the next half an hour devising an interview strategy for Gareth and Brett Carsons, before deciding the brothers would be surveyed before any interviews or arrests were to take place. The intention was that both could be apprehended at the same time, without warning or the opportunity to pre-warn any associates.

"We need to keep the brothers apart so that they cannot confer. Most importantly, they must not know why they have been asked to come to the station. Use the pretence of trying to locate Kai Masters. Focus on Gareth Carson's relationship with Asli Rahim, give the impression we are simply hoping they will assist us. We will feign ignorance of their connection to any trafficking crime until we can present them with evidence that we can use against them. DI Hammond will be present at the final interview for the Challenge Phase."

Hammond couldn't disguise anticipated satisfaction spreading across his face at DCI Hunt's words. How Brett Carson must have laughed at Hammond's gullibility when he pretended to be the simple, innocent employee caught in a turn of events beyond his control. Brett Carsons was the worst kind of criminal. Clever, devious, and one heck of a good actor. The day Hammond could expose him would be a very good day indeed.

Individual duties were delegated to other members of the team. As he watched Dunn and Edwards leave to begin their surveillance on the Carson Brothers, he felt a twinge of envy. He would have preferred to join them instead.

DCI Hunt finished issuing orders to the rest of the team then gestured to Hammond.

"I read your report. It was interesting." He referred to Hammond's long e-mail detailing all that he had hypothesised with Edwards the previous evening.

"The forensic data should confirm one way or other. And the interviews, of course."

Hunt pulled his tie looser around the neck. "I agree. I will push for the results." He changed the subject. "Your visit to see Bradley Kelsey has been scheduled for this afternoon. I want to run by a few details first to ensure you know what to ask him."

*

Hammond was restless. The drive had been quicker than he had anticipated, despite the queue of traffic held up on the M20 heading out of Maidstone. But as soon as he drove over the bridge to the Isle of Sheppey, his stomach began churning. He stopped at the petrol station and bought himself a milky coffee, hoping it would help him relax, but the adrenalin was pumping through his veins.

The prison car park was empty apart from a few vehicles parked in the shade at the other side, so he sat in the car waiting for his mind to become clear and focused. Every so often his mobile phone alerted him to incoming messages: Oxfordshire Police had the forensic results from the samples taken off the dead woman found in the woods. An email had been sent and was awaiting his attention. It was encouraging, but he refrained from reading the report. He couldn't process information when his mind was muddled with the thought of meeting Kelsey again. He felt he was wasting time. Bradley

Kelsey had been incarcerated over two years ago. Hammond didn't understand why it was necessary to churn up the unsavoury past. Despite Kelsey's hatred for him and the numerous attempts the man had made to kill him, Hammond did not fear him. It was likely their meeting would be supervised by prison officers, and therefore he would not be in danger, but he did not want to confront Kelsey either.

There remained many unasked questions that Kelsey had never resolved, including how he had managed to free a hand from the handcuffs during his arrest. After having lain dormant for so long, now the need for answers was stirred within him. But Hammond knew any attempt to provoke Kelsey was futile. He sat in the car for what seemed an age whilst the thoughts played on his mind. Eventually, he coerced his body out of the car. *I have to do it*, he thought. *I don't really have a choice.*

*

The prison guard was struggling. He breathed with short gasps that synchronised with his plodded pace as Hammond was guided along the corridor towards the room where Kelsey was waiting. After every so many metres, the man stopped. He pulled himself up at the chest and slid his index finger inside his trouser waistband and around his corpulent belly, wincing with discomfort at the pinch before resuming the walk. By the time they arrived at the visitors' meeting room, Hammond was relieved he hadn't needed to administer first aid. Although every police officer had to be competent in basic first aid, Hammond would be clueless if someone were to combust in front of him.

The guard bowed acknowledgement to Hammond's polite thank you and backed out of the room. The sound of the door being locked was heard, then silence as Hammond faced his former nemesis.

Up until that moment, Hammond's brain had registered he was about to embark on a potentially stressful situation. It had done what it was programmed to do, releasing epinephrine which caused Hammond's heart rate to increase, his lungs expanded fully to take in more oxygen, his pupils dilated giving optimum vision, and he began to sweat, keeping him cool in case he needed to flee the scene quickly. Hammond became aware that his heart was pumping louder. It was a common misconception experienced during anxiety. In reality, all that was happening was that the flow of adrenalin had exited his internal organs and he was experiencing intensification of his body's normal functions. Which is why, as he faced the man who had hated him so vehemently, Hammond started to giggle.

It started as a chuckle coming from the back of his throat – a nervous laughter that made his neck stiffen and his head loll backwards slightly – but as his eyes registered the grey, weedy looking man before him, the giggle became a chortle, then a guffaw, progressing into a loud hee-haw that echoed around the room. Hammond's body shook and rolled, his shoulders now bent down with the force of the laugh that was expelling from his stomach, tears began to stream down his face, and then he farted, which caused him to become hysterical.

He became aware of the door being opened and hands grabbing his elbow. Voices were agitated, and then a plastic beaker was forced into his hand. Eventually, he was able to control his body enough to take a swig of water, then he sat down, closed his eyes, and forced himself to take deep breaths. Silence ensued for a minute before he opened his eyes and looked into the hardened face of Bradley Kelsey.

"Hello," said Hammond.

From that moment on, Hammond didn't stop talking. He told Kelsey that prison appeared to have done wonders to the man's appearance. Aside from the shock of grey thinning hair that replaced the dark, curly abundance from previous years, Kelsey had lost a significant amount of weight. He had once been flabby but strong; now he was lean and fit. Probably just as strong, though, Hammond had offered as an afterthought.

He told Kelsey about why he was there, how intrigued he was that Kelsey had managed to slip out of the handcuffs that DC Michael Galvin had attempted to restrain him with. He didn't expect an answer so didn't pause to allow one. Instead, he rambled on as if he were entertaining a family member lying listless in a hospital bed. All the while, Kelsey didn't utter a sound. He just stared at the enthused policeman before him. Hammond talked for ten minutes without stopping, but eventually he paused.

"So, Mr Kelsey. How would you like to co-operate with me in exchange for some information that may interest you?"

Kelsey blinked, still silent but evidently interested in what Hammond could offer.

"That is, after all, why I am here. I cannot tell a lie, there would be no reason to visit you otherwise. But I am guessing you don't get many visitors, so perhaps you are a little bit pleased to see me after all these years, even if I am not the ghost that you had wished me to become once upon a time." Hammond's tone wasn't sarcastic. He sounded friendly, and noticed it was beginning to un-nerve Kelsey.

There was a surprising sense of elation bursting from within, and it drove Hammond on, all the while knowing it was unsettling the other man. From the moment Hammond had entered the visiting room, there had been a power shift. Kelsey probably still felt hatred towards Hammond, but it did not pose a threat. Instead, it was a source of energy, one that Hammond became intent on manipulating for his own needs.

"We are interested in a former acquaintance of yours. We believe he was a former client of Patricia Goodchild." Hammond spoke the name of Kelsey's lover slowly and with precision, all the while maintaining eye contact with the man he knew had been obsessively in love with his mistress.

"However, please don't worry, I am not referring to her clients from when she was a prostitute. Although, maybe they had known each other then as well..." Hammond exaggerated a thoughtful expression, aware that Kelsey had shifted in his chair.

"Get on with it." It was the first time Kelsey had spoken to Hammond. His voice was deeper than his appearance suggested it would be, yet it had the tone of a mopish, tired individual.

"There was a financial transaction made between you and Gareth Carson. You paid in cash for a second-hand, high performance vehicle in 2010, but immediately sold it and arranged for the funds to go to Gareth Carson."

There was no change of expression on Kelsey's face from hearing the latter name, but Hammond paused anyway, indicating he was expecting a reply.

"So?"

"So, it's odd. Very odd. Especially considering Gareth Carson's love of gambling. No pound was safe in his hands, was it? Look at the mess he made of his father's business! It was just as well big brother Brett stepped in and took over!"

The subtlest flinch shot across Kelsey's face when Hammond had mentioned Brett Carson. It was significant progress, enough for Hammond to pounce.

"Brett Carson is, as I am sure you are aware, a very naughty boy. He has been under the watchful eye of those people high up in the tower of Law Enforcement for a while now." Hammond raised an eyebrow. He hadn't offered anything more, because he didn't have anything to give; all he could do was bluff. But surprisingly, it was enough.

Kelsey coughed and shuffled in his seat a little. "So, what do you want?"

"I want to know everything that happened between you, every business transaction, and every conversation. When your darling Patricia left you, she took the business with her, didn't she? But she didn't retain Brett or Gareth Carson as clients. Why?"

"She died."

Hammond allowed a laugh.

"No, Mr Kelsey, you and I both know she is alive and well, and carrying on like before."

He stared at Kelsey, defying him to deny the knowledge. Kelsey stared back. He did not look surprised. But then, in a moment of long delayed clarity, Hammond remembered a scene from years ago. He and Detective Sergeant Tom Edwards had forced themselves into the apartment belonging to Bradley Kelsey. The search had been fruitful and they had found some evidence that had assisted with their investigation, but they had also noted a disturbed drawer in the freezer compartment. Ice had formed around unidentified objects that had been removed, so only imprints had remained. They hadn't identified the objects, but now Hammond realised what they had been.

"You froze Patricia Goodchild's blood with the intention of faking her death, but it went wrong, didn't it? You had to remove the stored transfusions quickly when my colleagues and I came to question you, causing the blood to defrost too quickly and destroy the blood cells. It was careless, but thankfully she wasn't aware of your mistake. So, as far as she is aware, she is believed dead and therefore is not of any interest to us any more." Hammond leaned forward and tapped the side of his nose with a wink.

"But she is wrong. Little does she know she is being watched very, very closely."

Kelsey could not hide the look of excitement.

"You know where she is?"

Hammond decided to lie. He nodded.

Kelsey looked at his hands, shifted in his seat, and looked at the prison guard standing solemnly by the door. "I need to know where she is."

Hammond faked surprise. "Why? She left you to get caught. You and I both know she had no intention of taking you with her. You had become a hindrance! For a start, you didn't kill me – which I am grateful for, by the way. I know you tried, but I am sure she didn't appreciate your constant mistakes. Then there was your interest in your daughter, which she didn't share; the clumsy murder of Patricia's former lover and adoptive father to your daughter..." Hammond paused, his eyes focused skywards, the index finger of his right hand tapping each of his left fingers as he ticked off the mistakes Kelsey had made whilst under the orders of Goodchild. "Well, it goes without saying that she grew tired of you, hence her running off without you."

Kelsey growled under his breath.

Hammond faked sympathy. "I understand what it feels like when a woman gets the better of you and, boy, she got the better of you, that's for sure! But she is devious; a cunning sociopath. You're better off without her."

"Tell me where she is!" Kelsey's upper body suddenly propelled forward, and he looked as if he would throw his body weight over the table towards Hammond. The man's eyes were now wide open, the man was enraged.

Hammond was ordered back as the guard attempted to hold Kelsey, who was now using his restrained arms as leverage towards where Hammond had retreated.

The guard had pressed the alarm, and suddenly there were several bodies pinning Kelsey face down on the floor. The man began screaming. Another guard ran in and gestured for Hammond to exit the room, but he hesitated. He spoke loudly over the ruckus to Kelsey, hoping that his words would be heard.

"I will come again. When I do, you will give me everything you know. In return, I will tell you where Patricia Goodchild is."

As he stepped out into the corridor, leaving the chaos he had created behind him, Hammond began to grin. He looked up at an imaginary cloud of heaven and saluted it.

"Almost there," he promised his dead former colleague, Michael Galvin.

CHAPTER SEVENTEEN

Hammond was back at the station by four o'clock. He checked DCI Hunt's office but it was empty, so he followed the sound of agitated voices coming from the briefing room.

"I cannot believe that you didn't check for any distinguishing marks in the first place!"

Hammond registered Acting Superintendent Brian Morris standing in the far corner with a reddened face. Directly opposite him was DS Lois Dunn, leaning against the desk as if she had lost faith that her legs would support her.

"Sir, we relied on information coming from his brother."

"Which is exactly why this investigation has gone wrong in the first place! Every detail had to be checked and checked again!" Morris stopped when he noted Hammond's entrance into the room. "Where the bloody hell have you been?"

DCI Hunt faked a cough. "Sir, I made you aware earlier that DI Hammond would be away from the office this afternoon." He threw a glance at Hammond before addressing the room. "We need to reissue another e-fit of Kai Masters. At least now we know about the tattoo, we can use it to our advantage. I am sure it isn't hard to miss, so the chances of Kai Masters being recognised have increased."

Hunt turned to Hammond. "Masters has a tattoo of the St. George's flag on the back of his head. Somehow we missed that when we began our search."

There wasn't a hint of blame being thrown in his direction, but Hammond felt shame at having missed such an important detail before. He was silent. Behind him, more people were entering the briefing room. Hammond looked at Hunt for an explanation for the increased activity.

"Kai Masters' van has been located overnight; it was discovered on a campsite between Canterbury and Sandwich, in an area popular for fishing. Initial reports are that it was found partly submerged in Victory Lake. I've just returned from the site, and have requested it to be processed as priority."

Hunt ignored Morris's mumbled comment and continued, "Officers are checking the local area, but it appears the vehicle had been intentionally rolled into the lake. It's probable that Masters left the area on foot."

Morris sighed and selected a chair. "The only reason we cannot openly declare Kai Masters as our killer is because British justice demands we give him the opportunity to prove his innocence. But in this case, I am inclined to believe he is guilty, which is why..." He sat down. "...it is essential he is apprehended without delay. We need to think like him, get inside his head; we know he is impulsive, irrational. If he dumped the van, it was probably a rash decision, in which case there could be some incriminating evidence close by."

Hammond interrupted. "Masters didn't take the van with him when he evaded arrest. He couldn't leave the premises by road. Our vehicles would have blocked his exit; he fled on foot." A moment of confusion unsettled him whilst he tried to remember whether the van had been in the vicinity when they had searched for Masters.

"Perhaps there is a back road?"

Hammond shook his head. "No. The whole area was searched. The only other exit was through trees that lined the perimeter between Nigel Berwick's property and his neighbour's garden. We're confident Masters was unprepared for our visit, but he had a couple of minutes to get away through the trees, following our request for entry into the grounds."

Morris's voice was gaining pitch. "Was the van there when you arrived?"

Hammond tried to visualise the scene "I thought it had been, but we would have confiscated it as potential evidence."

"The only other explanation is that he must have left the van elsewhere and returned to it, then abandoned it when he could continue by other means."

There was a patronising edge to Morris's manner, and Hammond felt he was being mocked. He knew it was unwise to continue, but there was a growing sense of unease building in his mind. Finding the van was progress, but it didn't fit somehow; it was almost too convenient. What it was that bothered him, Hammond couldn't say.

"Do we know when the van was abandoned? We have been looking for him for five days. Surely he would have travelled a distance away until it was safer to return?"

"Unless he is being helped." Morris's voice was clipped. "Check the brother; the grounds need to be searched again. Try to establish where the van had been kept prior to the attempted arrest." Morris turned his attention to Hunt. "I want a full team debriefing first thing in the morning," he barked as he exited the room.

But Hammond was distracted. He was trying to remember where he thought he had seen the van at Nigel Berwick's place, but all he could recall was having seen Kai Masters arrive during the first occasion he had interviewed Berwick.

Lois Dunn came forward and smiled a belated greeting at Hammond.

"How did it go with Kelsey?"

He shrugged, but then allowed the smile to creep onto his face. He explained the previous events in brief, enjoying the amused expression on her face as he recounted his flatulent episode.

"I left him screaming," he explained.

Dunn frowned. "Screaming? That seems a bit extreme for a man like Kelsey."

Hammond went to reply, but Hunt appeared beside her and immediately Dunn's attention shifted elsewhere.

"Oh dear." She addressed Hunt. "That didn't go well." She sighed as she removed one shoe and began massaging the arch of her foot.

"Mistakes have been made. It is inexcusable, but we can recover this investigation, so we will," DCI Hunt offered some consolation. He studied Hammond and Dunn for a moment. "Both of you need to go through all your notes, starting from the beginning of this investigation. Refresh your memories until you get every detail clear, and be ready for an early start. We must talk to Nigel Berwick again. Tomorrow, pay him a surprise visit and bring him in for formal questioning. If he is hiding anything, a surprise interrogation may work in our favour. From now on, we treat him as a potential suspect. He deliberately withheld information about his brother that could have aided our search. If necessary, we will use that against him."

*

Hammond worked until late, going over every note taken since he had interviewed the person he had believed to be David Hargreaves. Although the death of the infant had been treated as a separate case, it was evident from the emailed reports he was receiving from DS Shepherd that the murders on Langdon Bay were connected. So far, he had only skimmed the contents, but the news was good; the DNA samples collected from the woman found in Oxfordshire had been compared to the infant thrown from the van in Ashford. They were a match. Mother and child could at last be reunited. The thought was overwhelming, and for a moment Hammond was lost in rumination. He hoped that the woman had not been aware of her child's fate, but either way, she must have known she was in danger. She must have been terrified.

A surge of anger arose in his chest, but he forced it down and continued skimming the reports, encouraged to read that other foreign samples had been discovered on the woman's clothing and body which were due to be compared with forensic evidence taken from the bodies found at Langdon Bay.

He reconsidered the notes on the Carson Brothers. Until the two men were questioned, there was not enough to go on. The suspicion that Brett and Gareth Carson had been buying refugees from first Bradley Kelsey and then Kai Masters was just that – a suspicion. Not unless there was enough incriminating evidence.

According to DCI Hunt, Gareth Carson's suspected money laundering had been investigated elsewhere, but there was no evidence that he was involved in illegally bringing migrants into the country; it was all circumstantial, and therefore unlikely any other charges other than fraud would stick. Every single detail in Gareth Carson's bank records would have been monitored. Every single card payment, every penny spent and earned over the last three years had been scrutinised in order to identify any rogue transaction. That meant that to prove his involvement with Kai Masters, tons of paperwork would need to be shared between departments, which Hammond considered unlikely. And even then, it would have to be meticulously processed again.

It was a huge demand on a team of 16 officers who were already working beyond their means. Their priority was to find Kai Masters and provide enough evidence for the CPS to allow him to be charged for murder. Any other crime, or people believed to be implicit with that crime, was secondary.

Hammond sighed and ran his hand through his hair. He hated the fact that he was only able to complete what he considered to be half an investigation. He brought his mind to a halt for a moment whilst he glanced back down at his notes. There was no mention of a van being at Berwick's property on the day of the attempted arrest of Kai Masters. He turned the pages back in his notebook until he read every note from that day. And then he saw what he had missed.

For a second, there was the temptation to act. But then he glanced at his watch and saw it was too late; it would have to wait until the morning. He turned off the computer, collected his notes, then realised he had forgotten to phone Paul.

*

For the first time since Kai Masters had been identified as the main suspect for the Langdon Bay murders, Wallace Hammond had a clearer picture of events. He said as much to the team the following morning as they settled down in the briefing room.

"The problem so far is that we have relied on logic according to the evidence that we have found, but this whole case has been random. All along, Kai Masters used the route of less resistance, even though he acted impulsively. We presumed that Masters had left the scene when we arrived to arrest him, because Nigel Berwick told us that was the case. But he could easily have been lying."

Hunt sighed. He was under pressure. He couldn't afford to make any more mistakes.

"He didn't give us an accurate description of his brother, but it doesn't mean he is dishonest. Why would he lie about when his brother had left?"

Hammond glanced at his notes. He had a good idea why Berwick had lied, but it was a gamble – one that he knew DCI Hunt would not be prepared to accept without evidence. So, instead of sharing his thoughts, he shrugged.

"Delaying tactics, maybe. Whilst we were occupied search-ing the grounds, Masters was already miles away."

Hunt rubbed his forehead, thinking. If Hammond had been a mind-reader, he would have seen Hunt debating how much longer he would be allowed to supervise the investigation without it being handed over. They couldn't afford more mistakes.

They had arrived for a seven o'clock start, and for the last two hours the team had re-evaluated every bit of evidence that could be used against Kai Masters. It would be enough to

SHOES ON A WIRE

challenge him in an interview, even if Masters were to refuse to comment. The van was still being processed for forensic evidence, but there was already enough to implicate their prime suspect. A pasty wrapper, ripped open at the corner, had been found stuffed inside the driver's door; pastry crumbs had been found on the seat and footwell, suggesting there had been single occupancy in the van at the time it was abandoned, or for some time before that.

Rope, gaffer tape, and unused plant ties had been found in the back of van. But what had been most significant was the floor. The plywood that had been laid as a base was stained in the far-left corner.

"The lake goes up to ten feet in places, so the van could have been hidden for long enough for such evidence to be destroyed. However, the mud was churned at the perimeter. Chances are the van needed to have been driven into the water, as the driver would have had less luck pushing the vehicle further in without falling into the mud himself. Either option meant that the driver would have left the scene soaking wet or muddy, so would have been obvious to passers-by. Therefore, it is possible that they gave up trying to submerge it as intended, in order to leave quickly and unnoticed."

Naomi Combes, the principal crime scene co-coordinator, had been debriefing the team on the events following the removal of the van from the lake where it had been found. Hammond studied her, initially interested in the intelligence she was sharing, but his interest soon wandered as he admired her physique.

He blushed when she turned and caught his eye, causing him to suddenly become interested in something outside the window.

"The stains on the floor of the van were not disturbed because the van did not sink enough into the water. Therefore, there was enough residue to process. Presumptive tests were positive for biological material."

"Blood?"

Naomi shook her head. "We need to confirm our findings, but testing for latent blood traces is extremely time consuming. This doesn't look like blood." They were referred to the photograph projected onto the white board. "My initial guess is that it is urine."

"Is there any way to determine when the van had been driven into the water?"

"Forensically speaking, no, other than it was recent, within the last three days or as near as. Pondweed had been disturbed, as had the vegetation at the entrance site, so if it had been longer there would be signs that the vegetation had recovered, but that would have taken more than a week."

Hammond sighed. "So, witness statements are the best indicator of time. What progress has been made as far as questioning any campers or regular fishing enthusiasts at the lake?" He addressed the room.

Dunn spoke. "The campsite was closed due to the facilities being refurbished for the last three weeks. However, the entrance gate had been left unlocked to allow access to service vehicles. It would have been easy for Masters' van to have been mistaken as one belonging to the contractors."

"In which case, why submerge it in the water? Why not camouflage it by parking it amongst the other vans?"

Hammond scratched his head. "Probably because the van wasn't taken there during the day; the attempt to submerge it was during a moment of opportunity. Who reported the van's discovery?"

"Carl Jordan, aged 56, a local man and a regular fishing enthusiast at Victory Lake. He assumed it was a dumped stolen vehicle. He'd visited the lake eight days previously. We are compiling a list of regulars at the lake, but it is going to take time to question them all."

"Time is what we don't have!" Hammond slapped his forehead in a moment of utter despair. The team was at an impasse. He immediately felt the sting and wondered if his forehead was reddening or, even worse, had a hand print stamped on it as he faced the team before him. Then he turned to Naomi Combes. "Is there anything else found on or in the van that could help us?"

She hesitated then responded, "The driver's seat had been moved recently. Even though the front of the vehicle had been submerged, most of the water had collected in the footwell and front dashboard, predominately on the passenger side. The area under the driver's seat was less compromised by the water. We found that the adjustment handle under the driver's seat had been lifted but had not been clicked into place properly."

Hammond arched an eyebrow. "Could it have been caused by the angle of submergence?"

Combes shook her head. "Unlikely, the handle needs to be lifted and then slight force applied, either pushing back or forward until the seat can be locked into place."

Hammond was hopeful. "Fingerprints?"

Combes offered a half smile. "We checked but didn't get much; the water didn't help. A partial print was taken but the clarity is compromised."

Hammond considered for a moment before he spoke. "Either way, it suggests that someone else other than Kai Masters could have been driving the van moments before it was abandoned. That only reinforces the theory that Kai may have been helped to abscond by big brother Berwick."

Edwards nodded. "It does add up. Certainly, there is enough to raise suspicions about his involvement in Masters' disappearance."

Hammond stood up. "I'd like to bring him in myself if that is ok." He thanked Naomi Combes for her input as she prepared to leave, but then a thought passed through his mind and he called her back. "The stain on the van floor. You said it could be urine, but what about amniotic fluid?"

She nodded. "Well, amniotic fluid is essentially the infant's urine, so yes, it's probable."

Hammond smiled. "Thank you," he said. "It makes sense."

CHAPTER EIGHTEEN

Unlike his former wife, the younger Wallace Hammond hadn't enjoyed crime fiction or spy thrillers. They often left his mind disorientated. There were too many red herrings or conspiracy theories for his liking. Many a time he had left the cinema, after accompanying Lyn to the latest paranoid thriller, with the urge to shake his head until all sense of logic and order had returned to the surface of his mind. Such was the unsettling effect of such dramas that he had ended up making excuses for not finishing a novel she had recommended or going to the cinema to see the latest conspiracy blockbuster. It had irked her, but then most of his other virtues had done the same eventually. Hence their divorce several decades later.

Hammond was reminded of these incidents whilst reflecting that his mind was as discombobulated as it had been following two hours of conspiracy immersion. The case had begun with one single component: a man identifying himself as a local office worker reported a baby being thrown from a van travelling towards Ashford. The baby had been killed, possibly by the fall, or had been dead before being thrown. The mother had been searched for, but not found. Hence the case had been put aside.

Then a second component had emerged: five supposed refugees, having sought their way onto British soil covertly, had been attacked and killed by an unknown assailant. One had survived and had provided information of the events leading up to the attacks. All victims, including three others, had been sold the guarantee of a new life in Britain, but then been betrayed and either killed or passed on to traffickers who had intended to sell them.

Then there was the third feature: a local pigment manufacturing company was suspected of being involved with money laundering and being complicit in previous dealings with identified human traffickers Bradley Kelsey and Patricia Goodchild. The same company was suspected of continuing their business dealings using other traffickers, but evidence was limited. Hence the need to interrogate Bradley Kelsey using information Hammond did not possess as bait.

It looked simple on paper – three circles at opposing sides of the page – but Hammond wanted to expose the connections between all three components. He drew a line from the first to the second. First connection: Brett Carson had used the identity of one of his employees to report the baby's death. Then a second line was drawn between the second and third component: Gareth Carson had recommended the employment of Asli Rahim – who later became the surviving victim found at Langdon Bay – to Nigel Berwick, the elder brother of the prime suspect of the murders. Another connection: Brett Carson and Gareth Carson had previous financial dealings with Bradley Kelsey. The line continued back to the first circle until it had formed another circle of its own.

Hammond studied the paper in front of him. He was missing something. The centre. There had to be a point of origin. A midpoint from where the components had evolved. He jotted the names of all people involved so far: Nigel Berwick, elder brother of the suspect; Asli Rahim, victim and employee of Nigel Berwick; Frank Sullivan, co-smuggler with Kai Masters and friend of Nigel Berwick; Gareth Carson; Brett Carson. His pen hovered above the page. Their connection to the cases was evident, but what was their connection to the people involved? Possibly Bradley Kelsey, but Hammond realised there was nothing to prove their affiliation with the others.

There was an accompanying pang of despondency as Hammond realised near-defeat. He contemplated his scrawling until he was distracted by Dunn.

"Nigel Berwick's solicitor has arrived. We can question him now."

Wallace Hammond shook the hand of the man seated opposite him with respect. He saw a man that was genuinely worried, who feared for the fate of his younger brother. He recognised the tired expression, the nibbling of the lower lip, the rubbing of fingers against palms, as nervous displays. The behaviour he was witnessing was no different than the despair of a loving parent wanting to protect their young from the harsh reality of an unforgiving world. But despite the empathy, Hammond had no patience for pretence. The interrogation had begun.

"Mr Berwick, you are aware that your younger brother, Kai Masters, is suspected of the grievous bodily harm and attempted murder of your former employee Asli Rahim and the murders of four other people."

Silently Nigel Berwick nodded.

In acknowledgement, Hammond continued, "You are also aware that the police are anxious to find Kai as soon as possible, to question him about his suspected involvement?"

Berwick nodded again.

"At the time of Kai's intended arrest by me and my accompanying officers, you promised full co-operation?"

"Of course I want to co-operate." Berwick spoke assertively.

"Good. We appreciate that." Hammond smiled. "So, may I ask Mr Berwick why you did not give us a full, detailed description of your brother for identification purposes?"

"I did."

Hammond glanced down at the notes he had before him. "Not quite. You confirmed that the picture shown to you was of your brother Kai, but you did not add any details when asked by my colleague if there were any other distinguishing features that would help to identify him."

"I'm not sure I understand."

Hammond studied Berwick momentarily. Had he detected a sense of relief in the other's man's tone? "You failed to mention the St George's flag tattoo that your brother has on his head."

"Well, I didn't think. I mean, it's on his head. If he grew his hair, it wouldn't be seen anyway."

Hammond acknowledged this with a faint smile. "Yes, but in the picture my colleague showed you, your brother has a shaven head. In his apartment, there were hair clippers left out, so presumably he prefers not to let his hair grow?"

"Yes, that's true."

"So, the tattoo would have been relevant information that you deliberately did not pass on to us."

"Ok. Yes. I made a mistake. I'm sorry."

Hammond smiled again. "Thank you. Now, according to your initial statement, you said that it was Kai who recommended Asli Rahim to you as a carer for your mother?"

"Yes."

"Do you know the name of the person who recommended her to him?"

There was a pause, a moment of hesitation, before Berwick shook his head. "No, he just said a friend."

"And yet, when we asked you if there were any friends that Kai may have gone to following his absconding, you said you didn't know of any."

"That's true, I don't. At least, he has never shared any information about his friends with me."

"But you do know Frank Sullivan?"

"Yes, he looks after my yacht for me when she is moored at Sandwich."

"Would you consider him a friend?"

Berwick hesitated. , He looked confused by the question. "Well, not as a friend, but we are friendly."

"And Kai is also friendly with Frank Sullivan?"

"I guess so. I don't know. When Kai has accompanied me to Sandwich Marina, they would have a friendly chat."

"You said you hadn't used your yacht recently, due to the cockpit filling with exhaust fumes?"

"Yes. That's correct. I thought that was why your officers had asked to look at the yacht, in order to verify that information."

"No, not quite, Mr Berwick. We have a copy of the receipt that we wrote to you. The yacht was being examined for traces of drugs. Your signature is here."

"Well, yes, but I thought that was just standard."

Hammond shifted his weight slightly. "Mr Berwick. I have no doubt that my fellow officers had communicated the reason for their request to look at the yacht. For the record, I shall confirm for your benefit that Frank Sullivan has testified that he and your brother Kai had attempted to smuggle drugs in your yacht without your knowledge. His attempt to hide the packages in the bodywork consequently caused the cockpit's ventilation to be compromised. However, this doesn't explain why you did not tell me when I first questioned you that the yacht was fully operational at that time, having already been repaired by Frank Sullivan. Why, at the time of our initial questioning, did you not share accurate information?"

Berwick glanced quickly at the solicitor beside him. "Well, I must have forgotten."

"Ok." Hammond paused for a moment. "Perhaps you can help us with another matter of confusion. You said that Asli Rahim was entitled to one full week's holiday every month whilst she was in your employment?"

"Yes."

"Yet you didn't mention the fact that she had been away longer than seven days when we found her?"

Berwick leaned his upper body forward, mimicking a person hard of hearing. "I'm sorry?"

"Asli had been kept in France against her will for several days before she was brought back to Britain as a hostage.

From what we have managed to ascertain, she would have been away for at least ten days, yet you did not report her missing when she failed to turn up for work at the start of the week."

Berwick frowned. "Well, I figured she may have wanted some extra time off."

"Did you attempt to reach her during this time of absence?"

"No."

"Why not?"

"I didn't want to be a harassing boss. I like her."

"Had she ever been away longer than a week without telling you in advance, previous to this occasion?"

"No."

"Were you not concerned for her safety?"

"Why would I be? She is a grown woman and I am not her keeper."

"But you must have been worried about who would care for your mother if Asli did not return? Surely you would have been at the very least annoyed that Asli had not contacted you or pre-warned you of any intention to stay away longer than intended, for your mother's sake?"

"Well, I managed."

Hammond leaned forward slightly. "I shall explain the source of my confusion, Mr Berwick. You employed Asli to care for your dependent, ailing mother. Her employment was necessary, yet you easily managed in her absence without arranging for alternative care or questioning Asli's absence. I understand that currently you still do not have a replacement for Asli at home. It makes me wonder why you needed to employ her in the first place."

Berwick shook his head. "I don't understand what you are implying."

Hammond spoke slowly. "We only have your word that it was Kai's recommendation for Asli's employment. Additionally, we only have your word that Asli was not employed to act as translator to assist in the illegal migration of refugees.

Neither do we have any evidence that supports your claim of ignorance in your brother's suspected illegal activities. In fact, Mr Berwick, your behaviour thus far has shown constant inconsistency, and comes across as suspicious."

Berwick's face reddened. The display of nervousness had gone and was replaced by an expression of anger.

"I have co-operated to the best of my ability. I have told the truth, and you have no reason to suspect me of anything illegal."

"Let us be very specific, Mr Berwick. I believe that you are withholding information about your brother's disappearance. I acknowledge that you have told me otherwise, but we have now established that you have a habit of not sharing all the information that you possess. So, I am going to share with you the intelligence we do have." Hammond displayed the photographs of Kai's car partly submerged in Victory Lake. "We have identified this vehicle as being Kai's. Initial examination of the van confirms that Kai had been driving this van prior to his attempted arrest, and also that the van had carried other passengers, possibly against their will. Forensic analysis can be processed on traces found in the vehicle, so it is only a matter of time before we can establish the evidence as fact.

"However, one matter of significance is that, shortly before the vehicle was abandoned, the driver's seat had been adjusted, suggesting that Kai had not driven his van into the water; it was someone else. Whoever it was would have exited the van and would have gotten wet, their footwear and their clothing would show distinctive environmental residue from the lake and surrounding area when forensically examined, and then there would be the question: why? The likely motive being that Kai was being helped to dispose of evidence, or his disappearance has been engineered by another party, eager to cover their tracks. Either way, once we find those clothes and footwear, it will incriminate that person immediately, and then hopefully he or she could explain their motive themselves."

"I don't understand what this has got to do with me. I have already said I don't know any of Kai's friends so I can't suggest anyone who was likely to help him dump his van."

"I understand. However, we have been granted a warrant to search your property whilst you are here, so we can start by possibly eliminating you from this part of the investigation."

Berwick shot forward. "You have no bloody right!"

His solicitor leaned forward. He consulted with Berwick, whispering in his ear for a minute, then addressed Hammond directly.

"May I ask on what grounds this search warrant has been granted?"

Hammond passed the papers across the table for the solicitor to read. The man consulted Berwick with the details.

"We believe that you are aiding a suspected offender. This is a criminal offence that, if you were proven to be guilty of, could mean you face up to ten years' imprisonment. We suspect soiled clothing linking you to the site where the van was deposited will be found on your premises, and if we are correct, we will have sufficient evidence to arrest you for acting with intent without lawful authority to impede the apprehension and likely prosecution of an offender suspected of murder."

"Without that evidence, you will have nothing."

Hammond's instinct was telling him to proceed. Berwick was right; there was no solid evidence to incriminate the man of anything yet, but there was the need for answers. One answer in particular. Hammond hadn't voiced his suspicion to anyone else, but he intended to find out whether his instinct was serving him as well as he hoped. He quickly changed tack.

"You mentioned Kai's mother left when he was 11 years of age?"

Berwick stilled as if he had suddenly hit the pause button. "Yes." His answer was slow and pronounced. His eyes now focused entirely on trying to read the detective seated opposite him, but Hammond retained a neutral expression.

"Your father passed away at St Margaret's' Care Home in September 1998. You were present at the time of his death, and were therefore able to identify him in your role as next of kin?"

"What the hell has that got to do with anything?"

"Please confirm if our information is correct, Mr Berwick."

"Yes, it's correct, but why are you dredging up the past? The death of my father is irrelevant to your investigation." Berwick referred to his solicitor for back-up as he spoke. The solicitor nodded in agreement.

Hammond offered an apologetic smile. "I am simply establishing facts, Mr Berwick. Your father's death was registered within 24 hours of his demise, and you then made arrangements for the funeral."

"Yes!" Berwick was quickly losing impatience. The man was reddening from the neck upwards, and looked as if he may burst with exasperation at any moment.

Dunn, seated beside Hammond, had remained silent, but even she looked as if she was tempted to interrupt his questioning.

Hammond paused for a prolonged moment. Then very calmly he explained his reasoning.

"All your father's dealings were registered correctly. His estate had been officially handed over to you, as requested in his will. His marriage to your mother, your birth, the birth of your brother, and your father's death were registered, as is legally necessary. There were bank accounts in his name, one in your mother's name, you have a bank account, and you pay your taxes. Therefore, I wonder, Mr Berwick, why there is no record of Kai's mother residing anywhere else in the United Kingdom following her departure in 1995.

"Her entry into the country was registered in 1985. We have found a copy of her residence permit, and she is named on Kai's birth certificate. But there are no official records of her having changed her name, or any records showing that Hiromi Wakahisa-Masters left the United Kingdom. There were no bank accounts in her name, and no property registered as her residence from 1995. So, where would she be? It looks as if Kai's mother didn't just disappear from his life. It is as if she disappeared from this existence altogether."

Hammond waited. The shock of Berwick's face was apparent. He was mute; his mouth attempted to form words that couldn't be spoken. Eventually, after a minute of silence, he blustered a reply.

"I have no idea where she is! She may have run off with the milkman, for all I care! What the hell has this got to do with Kai?"

Hammond looked steadily at Berwick. He prolonged the gaze, telepathically communicating with the man opposite. Hammond now knew his instinct had served him correctly; he had no doubt. Berwick avoided Hammond's stare, and instead glanced at the solicitor and Dunn before Hammond spoke again.

"Well, Mr Berwick, perhaps there is a possibility that Kai was helped to abscond by his mother? You say you have no idea where he is—"

"No, I don't!"

"Well, then, perhaps Kai has learnt how to disappear from public scrutiny the same way as his mother?"

Berwick shot a quick glance at Hammond. "If that is what you think, then I guess you will have to prove it."

Hammond smiled, but kept his eyes trained directly on Berwick.

"I intend to," he said.

CHAPTER NINETEEN

Unforecast rain drizzle had lined the pavements with a soft sheen. It was lunch hour in the centre of town, and office workers were leaving their work places in teams of threes and twos. Their summer attire was not suited to the moisture that caused shirts to cling to the backs of men. A group of young women squealed as the wheels of a passing car splashed a puddle over their feet. One woman held a magazine over her head as an inadequate umbrella, and smiled apologetically as she bumped into the man standing by the bus stop alongside the office building. In response, Detective Constable Mark Ellis murmured a polite reassurance, and moved back slightly to allow more room on the pavement for the hurried pedestrians eager to make the most of their free time.

Despite the temporary distraction, his eyes did not waver from the middle-aged man who had, a quarter of an hour earlier, entered the café opposite. He was now seated alone at a table with his back to the window. Brett Carson had ordered a coffee and toasted sandwich, and was now sipping his drink whilst occupied with tapping on the screen of his mobile phone. It was the same routine that had been seen since surveillance had begun two days earlier.

Brett Carson appeared to be a hard working man who arrived at the office by eight in the morning, would remain in the office building until past midday, then drive the five minute journey into town and park in a space behind the café. By ten minutes past one, he would be seated in the café eating his toasted sandwich.

There was a queue in front of the counter; the café was quickly filling up with customers, causing the windows to become less transparent from condensation. Ellis moved quickly across the road until he was directly outside the window where Carson was seated on the other side. He hesitated, and then decided to enter the café where he could survey his mark easily.

Ellis ordered a coffee and sat on a bar stool as close to Carson as he dared. Half an hour later, the man stood up from the table and left the café. Ellis watched as he returned to his silver Mercedes, then phoned his colleague to take over the surveillance.

Nothing particular happened that afternoon. Brett Carson arrived back at his office building and did not emerge again until five. Less than an hour later, Detective Sergeant Tom Edwards joined the detectives parked on an industrial site a few metres down from a snooker club where Brett Carson had just met his brother, Gareth, and the two of them had entered the building. Five minutes later, Gareth came out the door and hovered outside, looking up the road. He checked his mobile phone then started punching a number. He scratched his leg and spoke several words into the phone.

"Is it worth me getting out and trying to listen?" One of the detectives turned to Edwards for guidance.

Edwards shook his head. "No, he is about to end the call. He's expecting someone. We'll wait and see who turns up."

"I'll go inside."

Again, Edwards shook his head. "No, it's members only, you may be too conspicuous. We'll wait a bit."

It was another 20 minutes before Gareth Carson was met outside the snooker hall by a weedy looking man in his late fifties. He wore a baseball cap, grubby jeans that hung from his hips, and a stained, lightweight anorak. He barely nodded at Carson as he approached, and concentrated on lighting a cigarette whilst Carson gesticulated impatiently. From where the detectives were situated, it was difficult to determine what was being said, but the meeting was short and at no time did the other man speak. He simply nodded occasionally and took regular drags from his cigarette whilst Gareth Carson talked. Then Brett Carson appeared at the top of the road, having left the snooker hall by the side exit. He watched Gareth and the other man from a distance before walking over slowly.

Edwards hissed to the officer in the driving seat. "Take a picture!"

Brett Carsons placed a hand on his brother's shoulder. Gareth stopped talking, then nodded and walked away, whilst Brett took something from his chest pocket and handed a small item over the other man.

"Zoom in, zoom in!" Edwards couldn't see what the item being exchanged was; only the camera may be able to help.

The exchange between the three men was short. The meeting had taken three minutes.

When the Carson brothers headed back inside the snooker hall, Edwards delegated the officer to stay where he was, then he left the car and followed the other man on foot. The man walked towards the main road, then crossed the street where a mobile catering van was serving hot drinks and burgers.

Edwards held back whilst the man ordered at the window, paid, and then sat on a low wall with his back to the main road. He ate his burger quickly and greedily, before throwing the paper napkin to the ground and standing up. He turned back towards where Edwards was waiting, and passed him without showing any awareness of his tail. Then he headed southeast towards the railway line and crossed over the footbridge.

Staying back as much as he dared, Edwards treaded softly on the steel steps so that his footsteps didn't reverberate on the bridge and draw attention to his presence. The man was gaining pace as he ventured past the old gas works and turned right. Several more turns, then he headed across the park. Edwards checked his watch. They had been walking several minutes now and he had no idea how much further they would be going.

They went through a housing development, then past an adult education college, before Edwards had an idea of where the man was heading. It was now more probable the man was heading home. About 40 minutes after Edwards had begun tailing his mark, the man approached a door to an apartment block. Pleased with himself, Edwards used his mobile phone to take a photo of the names listen on the mailboxes, made a note of the address, and then called to be collected.

*

Hammond had left work as early as he could, with a desperate need to sleep. The exhaustion that weighed him down was as much emotional as it was physical. The feeling of helplessness was overwhelming. The case was making no progress, and every time it seemed as if an obstacle had been lifted, more distractions were placed in their stead.

He had driven home distracted, and would have overshot the junction if the car behind him had not honked their horn at his near mistake. He thanked them by raising his hand in front of the rear-view mirror and slowed his pace whilst he searched for a parking space near to his apartment. When he did find one, it was several streets away, and the walk to his front door seemed unnecessarily prolonged.

Inside, he kicked his shoes off with the usual careless manner and proceeded into the kitchen, noting how stuffy the air was. He opened the window and leant against the sill for a moment whilst he deliberated whether to bother making a meal or settling for a cereal bar before bed. When his mobile vibrated in his trouser pocket, he groaned. He glanced at the screen, not recognising the number, but answered it anyway.

"Oh, good. I've finally got you!" The voice was female and familiar.

"Lyn? Is that you?"

"Good to know you still recognise me, Wallace. How are you?"

Hammond cradled the mobile against his ear, aware that he was shaking slightly. He hadn't spoken to his former wife for almost a year. "I'm good, you?" There was a moment of awkwardness whilst he struggled to think of something to say.

"I'm stressed. I'm trying to organise the seating plan and I need to know whether you are coming to the wedding and the reception, or whether you are intending to sneak out the back of the church during the ceremony, before anyone notices."

Hammond hesitated. "I'm not sure..." He left the sentence hanging. He wanted to tell her he didn't intend to go to the wedding at all, but something, maybe a moral conscience, stopped him.

"I need you to be sure, Wallace. If I put you near the head table, then I need to be sure you are going to be there, otherwise an empty seat would look too obvious."

"Ok."

There was a sigh. "Ok? What does that mean? You'll definitely be there?"

Hammond nodded into the phone. "Yes, I'll be there, Lyn. It will be an honour."

Lyn sighed with relief, He imagined her standing tall and erect, one hand resting on her forehead. It was a pose she had adopted even before they had met. Whenever she had reason to think, she always placed the palm of her hand against her forehead as if easing the pressure of mental strain.

"Will you be bringing anyone?" Her voice changed slightly; she was trying to be tactful.

"No, just me."

"Ok, great. In that case, I will put you next to Aunt Dora. I know you always found her annoying, but she is so deaf nowadays that she won't be able to eavesdrop like she used to."

"Can't I sit near Paul?"

"But he's on the head table with Cameron and me."

"Of course, yes, that's fine. I'm looking forward to it."

"No you're not, Wallace. You never were a good liar. Paul told me you weren't intending to come."

Hammond was about to mention demands at work, but commonsense prevailed, so he apologised and asked how the preparations were going. He didn't really care – preferably, he wouldn't want to know about the wedding at all – but Lyn didn't deserve him to be unkind.

She replied with enthusiasm, "It's going wonderfully well. Everything is more or less sorted already. I'm getting excited now. Only three weeks to go!" She did sound excited. It hurt.

He ended the conversation as quickly as he could and repeated how much he was looking forward to the wedding. She laughed, reminded him to look after himself, and hung up.

Dinner was forgotten. The mobile phone stayed nestled against Hammond's ear for a prolonged time whilst he digested her words. His eyes were fogged with the sudden onslaught of moisture, and he told himself to stop being pathetic before he shuffled off to bed like the broken man he had become.

*

"Just because he entered the building doesn't mean he is a resident." Dunn ventured an opinion.

"Either way, it is the only event of interest that has taken place after two days of surveying the Carsons. They haven't met anyone else other than this man, and we haven't the time or resources to waste. It's worth a look."

Dunn nodded obediently. She scanned the residents' names listed on the mailboxes that Edwards had provided. There were ten in total. After several seconds, she called out for his attention.

"Your photograph isn't the best, the man's features are hidden by his hat, but I think we have found our man: Tymek Mural, Polish national. Listed as resident at Stanhope Court, he was arrested in 2012 for affray, first offence. He threw a punch at his employer whilst being intoxicated... oooh..." Dunn looked up and smiled. "Now this is getting interesting... Tymek was released without charge following his employer's assurance that he was of good character." She raised her eyebrows and teased Edwards with an exaggeratedly mysterious expression.

Edwards sighed. "Get on with it! Is it something or not?"

"Oh yes!" Dunn grinned and slapped him hard on the arm. "Tymek Mural was employed at Berwick Industrial Waste Services from December 2011 until April 2014."

"Berwick, as in Nigel Berwick?" Edwards offered a laugh. "Good God, we're getting somewhere!"

Hammond arrived soon after, and was sensitive to the fact that the atmosphere was one of heightened enthusiasm. Edwards explained the recent findings as they ventured towards Morris's office. Earlier that morning, Hammond had been summoned, and now he welcomed the fact that Edwards had good news to share to their superior officers.

Hunt was waiting with Morris and smiled warmly when they entered. It was slightly un-nerving to Hammond who had gotten used to the stressed expression on their faces recently.

Morris listened to the update and nodded. "Yes, it's good, but we are no closer to arresting Kai Masters. Until we receive the forensic report on the clothes that were seized from his brother's place, we cannot provide an explanation for his whereabouts, which is making us look incompetent to say the least. Any suggestion that there is a multiple murderer on the loose is disconcerting to the local public, which is why I am refusing to release any further information to the media." He stopped talking, aware that he was repeating words already spoken days before.

"Have we enough to arrest Brett and Gareth Carson yet?" Hunt spoke up. He was sitting beside the window where the light was flattering to him, reminding Hammond of a male cologne advert he had seen on a billboard.

Hammond shrugged. "We can only ask for their assistance with our enquiries, which I am more willing to attempt now we have a link between the Polish man Edwards has identified.

We can see that there is a connection between Tymek Mural and Nigel Berwick. Tymek evidently knows the Carson Brothers, and we know that Kai Masters has an association with Gareth Carson, so there is a connection. But at this time, we cannot prove whether that connection is relevant."

Hunt considered, "What about Bradley Kelsey? He hasn't given anything yet. If he knows something that he can share, it will help us even more."

Morris nodded. "I agree." He gestured to Hammond. "I'll get you a visiting order as priority. This time, don't leave until you have information."

Hammond swallowed. "In that case, I need to know where Patricia Goodchild is."

Morris looked haughty at the suggestion. "Goodchild's whereabouts has not been shared with us. She is not our concern any longer. You can bluff."

Hammond stepped forward. "With respect, sir. No, I cannot simply bluff. I need to exchange accurate information in order to ensure we receive the same."

He stood his ground whilst Morris attempted to stand him down. Eventually Morris shrugged. "I'm not promising anything. Either way, prepare to go back to the prison this afternoon." He turned to Hunt. "We'll politely and respectfully ask the Carson brothers to assist us with our enquiries at their earliest convenience. The interview strategy needs to be prepared with precision and skill, which is why I am only allocating you with it. I may want to join you in the interviews."

Hunt nodded. As they ushered themselves out the door, Hammond had the unnerving feeling they were preparing for war.

*

The photographs that Edwards had taken the previous day were enlarged on the screen. Despite playing about with the images' resolution, the item that had passed between Brett

Carson and Tymek Mural remained a mystery. Hammond and Dunn squinted at the screen.

Hammond stretched to his full height. "Perhaps it would be worth watching Tymek for a bit, get an idea of what he does during the day, who he associates with. It can't hurt."

"We need to compile our reports and all the forensic data that has come in. I was hoping to sit with you both and compare notes, but if you're not here this afternoon then I guess I can wait." Dunn smiled encouragingly.

Edwards leaned on the table. "We are up to our necks in reports and data, but I haven't felt we have made any progress until now. We've been on a treadmill; we've put the spadework in but haven't actually got anywhere!" He sighed and looked up at Hammond. "Do you want me to come with you to see Kelsey?"

"Nice gesture, but one I must refuse." Hammond thanked him. "I'm not sure I will get anywhere, but you never know. He was in such a state when I left him that I'm not sure what to expect."

He noted Edwards' look of enquiry so recounted the details of his previous visit to Bradley Kelsey.

"Perhaps he was in pain," Edwards suggested when Hammond mentioned Kelsey screaming.

"As in heartache for Goodchild?"

"Maybe, or simply exasperation. He was betrayed by her, after all, which I suspect you took pleasure in reminding him."

Dunn scratched her head. "I don't think a couple of years would have softened that bastard one bit. Heartache can't be felt if you don't have a heart to begin with. I expect a guard simply kneed him in the balls or something when Kelsey was restrained."

Hammond turned to leave, but then a thought caused him to stop and address his colleagues. "Circulate Tymek's photo to the Ashford Vehicle Hire Company. Their description of the rental driver fits Tymek, and of course there is the photo ID that they copied. If he is the driver of the Vauxhall Combo from where the baby was ejected, we've got something."

He left the office reluctantly. Once the thought had entered his mind that Tymek was the missing link, he wanted to stay and pursue the enquiry himself. A feeling of optimism was beginning to stir within him. For a brief second he crossed his fingers and muttered a wish.

*

Hammond's excuse that he needed to leave early to drive to Sheppey because of possible road works had been weak, but thankfully it had gone unnoticed. Instead, he had spent some time in the private confines of his car using his mobile phone's internet search app. The research had taken longer than he had anticipated but it had proved worthwhile, despite having arrived ten minutes later than his visit had been scheduled. Hammond's tardiness didn't go down well, and was made worse by his demand to see the prison doctor before he met Kelsey. The request was unexpected and therefore ruffled a few feathers within the prison staff, but nonetheless his wish was granted.

"I cannot and will not breach my patient's confidentiality," the doctor spoke stiffly, clearly unimpressed by Hammond's brazen attitude.

"What if your patient had already told me about his condition and I simply need you to confirm it?" Hammond was pushing his luck.

The doctor eyed him before asking. "Has Mr Kelsey told you himself?"

"Yes." Hammond used an assertive tone. He wasn't lying; not as such. Kelsey had certainly shown certain characteristics that had told Hammond something, but it wasn't quite clear what that something had been. However, Google had helped, and all he now needed was confirmation.

He waited, aware that he was being scrutinized, but eventually the doctor answered. She sighed and gestured for him to sit down beside her.

"I need Mr Kelsey to give me permission to disclose his details. However, knowing that this particular patient is not the most communicative or the most compliant, I shall give you the benefit of the doubt." She paused. "I can confirm that Mr Kelsey had been diagnosed before his incarceration, and I have taken on the responsibility of continuing his treatment."

Hammond stood up and shook her hand, trying not to show the euphoria he was feeling. He nodded to the guard and followed the man towards where Kelsey was waiting.

CHAPTER TWENTY

Hammond did not enjoy being deliberately dishonest. Implying the truth, as he had to the doctor, was a lesser sin because it had been necessary and it hadn't been a blatant lie. But now he was faced with a dilemma. He had promised to share with Kelsey information about Patricia Goodchild's whereabouts. It wasn't possible, so he did the next best thing.

"When Lloyd Harris asked me to investigate Goodchild's former adoptees, he shared information about her. A lot of it was not relevant as evidence used to incriminate you, so I held onto it. It may be useless, but this is what I am offering you instead."

Kelsey leaned forward. "That is not what you promised me."

"No, but there may be clues as to where she went. There may be a pattern of behaviour that you can identify."

Kelsey moved to get up, and immediately Hammond reacted; he couldn't afford to lose his chance.

"I can offer you something else," he said.

Kelsey paused. His expression was one of scepticism. "You know what I wanted. There is nothing else you can give me."

Hammond held up a hand. "I know you are in constant pain, that your condition is worsening. I know that you are often fogged with medication. If you co-operate with me just this once, I will do what I can to recommend you be moved to somewhere more comfortable."

Kelsey sat down again. "What do you know?"

"I know how you slipped out of the handcuffs when we arrested you. It wasn't human error, like I originally supposed, it was your joint hypermobility – a symptom of Ehlers-Danlos Syndrome."

Kelsey said nothing. Instead, he surveyed Hammond for a moment as if considering his options.

"Your recommendation cannot guarantee I will be moved."

Hammond agreed. "No, but I can promise to show how you have co-operated willingly; that will help."

Kelsey looked down at his hands whilst he contemplated the offer.

Hammond waited nervously. He remembered the feeling of power he had enjoyed on his previous visit, but now the situation had reversed. Kelsey had regained control.

Eventually the prisoner nodded. "Ok," he said.

Hammond exhaled then smiled. "Good," he said. "Now, what can you tell me about Gareth and Brett Carson?"

*

Kelsey talked. His narration was clear and concise. Robert Carson's pigment manufacturing company created natural and synthetic inorganic pigments and automated pigment handling systems used by manufacturers of colourants, plastics, and other industrial uses. The company had been built on Carson's flawless reputation as a fair, generous employer. He had often stated his intention that the pigments he created were to be manufactured using the most environmentally sound methods, with the ambition to evolve into manufacturing organic pigments.

When Gareth Carson took over the business following his father's death, he was already in debt through gambling. He paid his debts using the business profits. In an effort to cover his rogue transactions, he compromised on the quality of the synthetic chemicals used in the manufacturing of the colourants. It was cheaper to use heavy metal salts which, although legal, were recognised as toxic. In an effort to minimise expenditure, the number of factory workers was significantly reduced.

Within months, numerous complaints of respiratory and dermatological problems were being reported by the remaining factory workers. Many of the pigments Carson Bros produced were sold to industries manufacturing cosmetics and pet foods. Carson was barely operating within the confines of the law, but the reputation that had ensured the business's survival was close to obliteration. If the company folded, more questions would be asked and the legal enquiries would be detrimental.

To prevent exposure, Brett Carson took over; he ensured that all staff were replaced with cheaper labour. The factory workers were migrants, many so desperate to work that they were not as concerned with health and safety regulations or possible carcinogenic effects. They knew what to say during inspections, they tolerated longer working hours and less pay, and knew when to look away.

"Look away?"

Kelsey nodded. "The disposal of toxic substances provided a risk. There was a need to dispose of the solvents discreetly."

Hammond suddenly understood. "Which is where Nigel Berwick came in?"

Kelsey nodded. "I don't think he was aware. His brother organised the waste disposal."

Hammond considered what Kelsey had shared. "I presume Kai Masters also organised the import of cheap labour in the form of migrants?"

Kelsey nodded again. "Not until we lost our business. Originally, Pattie and I supplied the first new workforce. We selected over 200 within a year."

"Did you approach them, or the other way round?"

"Gareth had a fondness for Asian women; Pattie supplied them. He got to know us through that. I presume she offered to supply the workers as well."

"Tymek Mural. Do you know him?"

Kelsey considered a moment then shook his head. Hammond showed him a copy of the photo, but he repeated the gesture. "No, I don't know him."

Kelsey's failure to implicate Tymek was disappointing, but Hammond was satisfied that the links were slowly connecting. Just as Hunt had predicted, it was a long chain.

"Kai Masters and Gareth Brett. How do they know each other?"

Kelsey scratched his chin and shrugged a shoulder. "I don't know. They probably met at a pub and became drinking buddies or something. Gareth was older, but he was immature. Pattie was interested in Kai at one time; thought he could be useful. But he was too idealistic and couldn't be manipulated so easily. That's all I know."

Hammond digested what Kelsey had shared. "You realise that you have implicated yourself by telling me this? You've admitted your involvement in trafficking and prostitution, to say the least."

Kelsey stared at Hammond. He seemed about to react, his shoulders had tensed, his breathing quickened.

Hammond held up a hand. "Relax. I am not threatening you. I am simply confirming that you have co-operated with me fully and I will note my appreciation on my recommendation."

"So, find me Pattie."

Hammond stood up. "I suspect it will be only a matter of time. Be patient. I made you a promise. If I find out where she is, I will tell you."

Kelsey nodded. He remained seated whilst Hammond waited for the door to be unlocked by the guard outside. Then he spoke. "The information that Harris gave you, I want it."

Hammond gestured a thumbs-up over his shoulder, then left Kelsey without taking another look.

*

Throughout the journey back to Folkestone, Hammond deliberately avoided thinking about work, and distracted himself listening to the *Jazz Suite* by Dmitri Shostakovich on the radio. Shostakovich was not a favoured composer of Hammond, yet he couldn't fail to notice how his body responded to the music, his hands miming a waltz against the steering wheel until he caught the bemused glance of a passing motorist.

The sky had retained its vivid summer blue. It was going to be another warm evening. Hammond fumbled for his sunglasses in the driver's door and settled back into his seat, humming merrily. By the time he reached the station, he felt revived.

His mood was lightened even more when he heard that Tymek Mural had been positively identified by the Vehicle Hire Company in Ashford. Dunn and Edwards had gone to Ashford to make the arrest. Whilst they waited for an update, Hunt called Hammond for a meeting in Morris's office.

It was evident that despite the team's recent lack of morale, progress had been made; pathology reports, forensic analysis data, and statements littered Morris' desk. He nodded a greeting as Hammond entered the room, and they began their update by discussing the events surrounding Kai Master's disappearance.

"I find it very odd," Hunt mused. "There has been no sighting of him at all; there has been no money withdrawn from his bank account; no credit cards used in his name, or his brother's, that could give us a clue. It makes no sense."

"He must have hitched a lift with a stranger. We've circulated his description to all the police and border authorities, so I'm sure we'll get him eventually." Morris was clearly embarrassed by the subject of an absconded suspect.

"The only other conclusion is that he has been helped in other ways," Hammond suggested. He explained his theory to the men who listened intently.

"It's a bit far-fetched," Hunt said, then looked at Morris contemplatively. "But I agree there doesn't seem to be another explanation."

"We have the analysis report regarding the clothes that were seized from Nigel Berwick's house. There were no clothes found that showed any traces of him being at the lake or anything that ties him to Masters' van, but they did find traces in the soles of his shoes. It is enough to bring him in again." Hammond smiled encouragingly. The three men agreed.

"The pathology report on the woman found in Oxfordshire has confirmed she died from heart failure, possibly caused by haemorrhaging during childbirth and her malnourished condition. She has been identified as the newborn baby's mother, but we have no way of identifying her since it cannot be confirmed where she had originally come from originally. The stain found in Kai Masters' van is a biological match. It is likely that her waters broke whilst she was being transported, then she gave birth during transit, after having been handed over. In addition, she had foreign fibres on her clothes that matched the clothing worn by one of the victims found on Langdon Bay, so we know that at some point they were confined together. It supports Asli's testimony." Morris looked up from the report he was reading.

"So, all we need is Tymek's testimony to confirm it and to implicate Brett Carson?" Hunt whistled between his front teeth. He stated with assurance, "I will interview him this evening."

Hammond considered the photographs of the victims before him. The sight of the young man with the missing shoes pulled at his conscience. "Have we made any progress in identifying the other victims?"

Hunt offered a reluctant nod. "According to Asli's statement, the female victim was known as Sakina, but we do not have a full name. All we know is that she was a refugee from Afghanistan. We found some personal items in the warehouse where they were held in France; some papers which we think are written in Arabic script are being translated, and another possible significant finding on one of the bodies that could help to name one of the males. The rest are likely to remain anonymous."

They talked through various aspects of the case for another hour, during which Hammond briefed them on his conversation with Kelsey. He omitted to mention how he had persuaded Kelsey to share the information; he simply did not have the energy to justify his handling of Bradley Kelsey.

The remaining tasks were assigned for the following morning before Hammond retreated to his own office and closed the door. Within seconds, he had retrieved his jottings from the previous day. He contemplated the three circles and then paused. Before he had mentioned it to Hunt and Morris, he been reluctant to share his instinct, since it was no more than conjecture. But he had a certainty where Kai was likely to be found, the question was why? He stared at the paper before him, but his mind kept returning to the missing centre.

Eventually, Hammond decided to have faith in what his instinct was telling him. In the middle of the circle, he wrote: Hiromi Wakahisa-Masters. 1995. Then he folded the paper into four, slipped it into his trouser pocket, and went home.

CHAPTER TWENTY-ONE

Wallace Hammond met Nigel Berwick's mother for the first time just after seven in the morning on the Thursday. She was petite, half the size of her son, and looked anxiously from the window. Berwick had opened the front door as the patrol car pulled up the driveway, and walked over to where Hammond had parked his car behind.

"Could you turn off the flashing lights?" Berwick asked. "They're making her nervous."

Hammond sensed the sadness in the man's voice. He forwarded the request to the Police Constable and followed Berwick into the house, the accompanying officers in tow.

"Do I need to call Social Services for Mum?"

"Do you have a designated carer or family who can care for her?"

Berwick shook his head. "No. Just me." He walked over to where his mother stood, her shoulders shaking. He draped a blanket over her and guided her to the armchair.

Hammond did his best to smile and appear reassuring, although it was evident Berwick had been expecting his arrest. Whilst the man settled his mother, Hammond waited by the door until Berwick joined him. Hammond reminded Nigel Berwick of his rights, the reason for his imminent detention, and the offer of legal advice. Berwick listened politely before requesting his solicitor to be present. Hammond agreed.

"I would take you to the station." Hammond explained. "But I think it is best that we meet your solicitor here. That way, you can show us all where Kai is."

Berwick nodded. The men did not talk again until the solicitor had arrived. In the meantime, Berwick's mother was being referred to a local care home. One phone call and already her future had been decided without any consultation.

Berwick had agreed to co-operate, and he kept his promise. Within hours, the forensic teams had been directed to the grounds behind the tennis courts. The area had been marked, photographed, and the excavation had begun.

"How did you know?" Berwick turned to Hammond. He had aged overnight.

Hammond shrugged. "I know you love your brother, but you couldn't protect him any more. This was your only option."

Berwick nodded, watching the activity in front of them. "I always loved Kai. But even as an infant he enjoyed hurting people. He never wanted cuddles or company. His mother was gentle and adored him, but he never showed her any love in return."

"What about your father?"

"Dad was different. He was a hard man, firm, sometimes cruel, but fair. I guess he wasn't really interested in being a father. He was an old-fashioned man; the women raised the children whilst the men brought in the money."

Hammond prompted, "Which is why you took on the responsibility?"

Berwick nodded.

"So, tell me about Kai's mother? Did he kill her?"

The man nodded again. "Kai was embarrassed by her. He hated the fact that she looked different, that she had an accent. The more she tried to please him, the more he despised her. I was aware of it, but it wasn't my business. My mother was my concern, and if I am honest, I resented Kai and his mother for having caused my mother to have been tossed aside the way she was. So, I ignored it, pretended it wasn't my problem. I pretended not to notice how Kai spoke to his mother, how he taunted her. Then, when I was away at university, my father called me and told me to come home immediately. I returned home to bury her."

"So, your father knew?"

"It was my father who insisted that the police were not to be informed. We agreed to say that Kai's mother had left. After that day, we never mentioned it." Berwick looked at Hammond. "It's strange. When you hinted that you knew, at first I panicked, wondering how you knew. I knew you wouldn't be able to prove it easily so in that sense I was reassured, but then there came a sense of relief. I wanted you to know. I didn't want to pretend any more."

"That's normal," said Hammond. "Why did you kill Kai?"

Berwick lowered his head, his shaking shoulders betraying the emotion he was battling with. "I have always believed that, in some circumstances, capital punishment is the only way to stop criminals. It is as if some people just can't help themselves. It is in their nature to destroy other human beings. They feel no remorse, just a need to keep inflicting torture. Kai was like that." He turned to Hammond. "The day you first came here, I knew that Kai was responsible for killing the people on the beach. I looked in his van; the smell was putrid. In his apartment, I found tide tables, a logbook, and the gun. I knew there wasn't any way to make him stop."

"So, what did you do?"

"I invited him to the house for dinner the evening after you and your colleague first interviewed me. I made him the best meal I could think of," Berwick scoffed quietly. "I ground some of Mum's hypnotic medication and mixed it with red wine. It put him to sleep quickly and painlessly, then I suffocated him."

Hammond breathed in the morning air until his lungs were full. The air was still damp and clean; the first days of autumn were approaching.

*

News of Nigel Berwick's confession and subsequent charge was put on hold whilst the forensic team excavated two bodies from the grounds of Elm Cottage. A skeleton, believed to be of a woman, needed to be processed before it could be officially declared as the missing body of Hiromi Wakahisa-Masters, but the body of Kai Masters had been formally identified. The preliminary examination of his body confirmed he had died from asphyxiation.

Upon arrival at the station, whilst Berwick's detention was being processed, Hammond had retreated to his office with a heavy heart. He thanked God that he hadn't had to deal with a son who had a personality disorder. He wondered whether he would have had the strength that Berwick had exhibited. Berwick hadn't killed because he wanted to gain. He had killed as an act of mercy. The thought of hurting Paul, even to protect him, was too terrible to bear. Hammond switched his mind off whilst he updated Morris of the morning's events.

His boss listened, then informed Hammond of other progress. "The interview with Tymek went well. Once Hunt started quoting forensic data at him and mentioning deportation, the man buckled. He confessed to working for Brett Carson, and has admitted dumping the body of the woman in Oxfordshire, but maintains she had died during transit." Morris sounded enthusiastic at the other end of the phone.

Hammond congratulated the success. "Has Tymek said whether the baby was dead before it was thrown from the van?"

"No, that bit remains unclear. Tymek claims he was driving and couldn't see what was happening in the back of the van. He only stated that he was given orders to dispose of the baby by Brett Carson."

"But is it enough to make a charge?"

Morris's voice had the sound of a man smiling at the other end of the telephone. "Well, he has told us where he dumped the hire vehicle. Once we recover it, it will act as sufficient evidence. At least the CPS are happy."

Morris continued, "So, you were right about Kai Masters being dead. That was a bit of luck!"

"And deduction, sir." Hammond was in no mood to be patronised.

"Yes, indeed." The conversation was brought to a close. "DS Dunn and Edwards are informally interviewing Gareth Carson, He has the impression he is helping with enquiries to find Kai Masters. I'm awaiting the results of their interview before DCI Hunt interview Brett Carson. With Tymek's statement, we may be able to go straight into interrogation phase, but I will allow you to enjoy challenging Brett Carson as we originally planned."

"Thank you, sir." The call was ended.

For the first time in weeks, Hammond was seeing a speck of light at the end of what had felt like a very long tunnel.

*

Gareth Carson appeared to be an amiable sort of man. He answered all questions politely and clearly, and gave the impression that he wanted to be helpful but simply did not have any information on where Kai Masters could be. He had displayed surprise at the suggestion that Masters was a suspect in a murder case, but was quick to add that he had not known Kai Masters as a friend, more as an acquaintance.

Edwards feigned surprise. "Oh, we were given the impression that you have known Kai Masters for several years, that you were friends."

Gareth looked at Edwards with a furrowed brow, then shook his head slowly. "No, that is a mistake," he said.

Dunn smiled. "You recommended Asli Rahim to Kai Masters as a carer for his stepmother?"

Gareth hesitated. "No, I don't think I did."

Dunn smiled again. "You did. Asli confirmed it, and so did Nigel Berwick."

"Oh. Well, maybe I did. I can't remember."

Gareth shifted in his seat. Edwards proceeded to make him more uncomfortable.

"You knew Kai well enough to know that his brother was looking for a carer?"

Gareth was beginning to tie himself in knots. "I like helping people," he replied.

"Did you recommend the employment of Asli Rahim?"

"I guess so."

"So, you can confirm that you know Asli Rahim?"

"Umm... not well."

"How did you become acquainted with her?"

Gareth was looking more uncomfortable by the second. From behind the two-way mirror, Hammond watched; the scene before him was almost entertaining.

"I can't remember."

Edwards leafed through the papers in front of him. "Allow me to remind you. According to Asli's statement, she met you in Paris. You taught her about English football and told her about London. You made it sound beautiful."

Edwards looked up and smiled. "It is beautiful," he agreed, before continuing to read from Asli's statement in front of them.

"I quote: 'Gareth told me that England is not like the Continent, I would need documents to get into the country, but he knew someone who could arrange to get me a Netherlands ID and a plane ticket to Glasgow'."

Gareth licked his bottom lip and shook his head again. "It must be another Gareth."

"You do not know Asli? Or she simply knew two men called Gareth from England?"

"I don't know her."

Edwards paused a moment. He looked at Dunn. She looked at him. Both wore confused expressions before Edwards turned back to Gareth Carson.

"You just said you didn't know her well. You didn't say that you didn't know her at all."

"Well, to be honest, I know lots of girls. I can't remember if I know someone called Asli or not."

"Would a photograph help?" Edwards shuffled through the papers and presented a photograph of Asli Rahim to Gareth. It was not the best picture. One side of her face was blistered and scarred.

Gareth swallowed. "No, I don't think I know her."

"Ok, but you do know Kai Masters?"

"A little."

"Have you ever worked with Kai, or been involved in a profit-making scheme with Kai?"

"No."

"So, was Kai mistaken when he thought you had recommended Asli as a carer for his stepmother?"

Gareth offered an attempt at a laugh, but it came out as more of a low yelp. "I guess so!"

"I admit I am a little confused, Mr Carson," said Edwards "In Asli's statement, she says that you paid for her bail as an immigration detainee, to allow her to claim asylum in Great Britain. As a result, she owed you, which is why you suggested that she took up employment with Kai Master's brother in order to pay off her debt to you."

Gareth shook his head. "I know Kai. I vaguely remember him mentioning that his brother needed a carer for his mother, so I may have suggested someone, but I can't remember whether I did or didn't."

Edwards smiled and closed the file in front of him. "Not to worry, Mr Carson. It will be easy enough to check out with the Immigrants Detention Centre where Asli was held. How about you take a break whilst we do a quick check?"

From behind the glass, Hammond smiled.

*

"We can't keep him waiting long," DCI Hunt advised. "Gareth Carson is here voluntarily. He is under the impression he is helping us to find Kai, not to be questioned on his relationship with Asli Rahim."

Edwards nodded. "Ok, what do you suggest?"

Hunt sighed. He wanted to go in for the kill, but he needed to question Brett Carson first. "Thank him for his co-operation and let him go."

Dunn protested, "But, sir, he couldn't look more guilty!"

Hunt addressed her. "We can't risk losing Brett as well. We have to let them think they've got away with it before we challenge them with the evidence."

Edwards sighed. "I understand, sir."

He accompanied Dunn back into the interviewing room, where he apologised for the delay and tried to adopt a casual demeanour. "Mr Carson, you have helped us with our enquiries and we thank you," he said, "but before you go, could you tell us where you were on the morning of the 18th August?"

Gareth relaxed. "Probably at home or at work. It would be easy enough to check."

"But as far as you remember you were not in the company of Kai Masters?"

Gareth replied, "No."

"Have you seen Kai Masters, or have you been in contact with him since 18th August?"

"No."

Edwards rose from the chair. He shook Gareth's hand, thanked him for his time, and watched him leave the station with the swagger of a guilty man who'd got off lightly.

*

In comparison to his elder brother, Brett Carson was cool and collected. Within seconds of being questioned, he was able to confirm that he knew Kai Masters; they had moved within the same social circles at some point and he was aware that his elder brother knew Kai. But their relationship was not close, therefore he was not able to help Kai be located.

When he was asked where he had been on the 18th August, he replied that it was likely he had been travelling to work.

When asked if he had stopped en-route, Brett Carson did not hesitate. He suggested he may have stopped for petrol, but that he did not meet Kai Masters.

The man might have been telling the truth. They had no evidence that Kai had met Brett for the handover. They could only prove that he was involved in the transportation of the migrants following the handover.

Brett Carson was relaxed, but his body hinted at impatience, that they were wasting his time. DCI Hunt must have noted it, too, because he chose that moment to begin interrogating.

"Kai Masters is suspected of murder. We believe that he is responsible for the assault and illegal trafficking of migrants."

Brett pursed his lips. "What has this to do with me?"

DCI Hunt leaned forward. "I am glad you asked, Mr Carson, because from our enquiries it appears to have a lot to do with you. Our investigation into Kai has exposed his operation which involved bringing foreign people covertly into England. We have a witness account that states on the 18th August Kai Masters brought a dinghy with eight passengers to Langdon Bay. We have another witness account that implicates Kai in holding some of these passengers against their will. Two others were taken away, including a heavily pregnant woman.

"During our investigation, your name has appeared several times, which suggests you may be involved or you may have some knowledge of Kai's operation. I would like to understand why you appear to be involved. And therefore, before I ask any further questions, I would advise you to seek legal advice."

The arrogance of Brett Carson superceded his commonsense. "I don't need legal advice. I haven't been accused of anything."

*

The hour dragged by. From behind the mirror, Hammond watched whilst the interrogation continued. After ten minutes of further questioning, Brett Carson had enlisted the help of his solicitor. Although he was granted permission to leave, Carson didn't call their bluff – much to the relief of Hammond. It seemed that the man was so arrogant he truly believed he could not be implicated in any crime.

He was asked about Gareth and his relationship with Asli Rahim, but Brett denied any knowledge of his brother knowing anyone with that name. He feigned ignorance when confronted with details about Gareth assisting Asli with the purchase of fake documents in order to enable her entry into Scotland. He denied any knowledge of Kai Masters' trafficking operation. When asked if he had been involved in trafficking, he replied with a short laugh, "Absolutely not."

"Did Carson Bros ever invest in any profit-making schemes run by Kai Masters?"

"No."

"Has Carson Bros employed illegal immigrants?"

Again, Brett Carson smiled and shook his head. Non-British personnel might be employed in his company, but no, not illegal immigrants.

"Have you ever made enquiries about purchasing foreign workers to be used as cheap labour?"

Brett Carson didn't flinch. Instead, he remarked to his solicitor that such questions were ludicrous and time wasting. Just because he had known Kai Masters, who was suspected of trafficking migrants, didn't make him guilty. The solicitor agreed and requested that the questioning cease until they had enough evidence to continue.

At this point, Hammond rubbed his hands together in anticipation. DCI Hunt asked whether Brett Carson would be kind enough to wait a while until they had concluded their interview. "There are only a few more questions to ask," he said.

Carson smiled and shrugged. He didn't seem bothered at all.

But his expression changed when he saw DI Wallace Hammond enter the room, even though he recovered quickly.

Hammond smiled a greeting and settled in the chair opposite the man he genuinely had been looking forward to meeting again.

"I must apologise, Mr Carson, but DCI Hunt has been called away. Therefore, I will be concluding this interview. I do wish to bring it to your attention that, following your earlier interview with my colleagues, you are suspected of being involved in criminal activity. Therefore I need to warn you that anything you say could be used against you in a court of law."

Brett sneered. "You're arresting me? On what grounds?"

Hammond leaned back. "Well, for a start, you gave false testimony at the scene of a fatal road traffic accident, which is akin to perjury. Let's start with that."

Brett Carson studied Hammond before answering, "I simply gave a different identity in the heat of the moment."

"Regardless of the understandable trauma you were experiencing at the time, you signed your statement, and therefore officially declared it as a statement of truth under the false identity of David Hargreaves. By doing so, you obstructed a police enquiry."

"Ok, I admit it was stupid. I hold my hands up for panicking, but that's all I am guilty of. You have nothing else against me."

Hammond raised his eyebrows. "On the 18th August, about an hour before your road accident, Kai Masters met the driver of a hired white Vauxhall Caddy at the services of Junction 11. The meeting had been pre-arranged, with the intention of handing over three unwilling passengers – one was heavily pregnant. In fact, during the journey from Dover, she had gone into labour. Despite this, she and the other passengers were moved into the hire vehicle. Their journey continued towards Ashford."

Hammond paused. Throughout his narration, his gaze had not left Carson's face once. The man remained silent, so Hammond continued.

"Just before 7am, the hire vehicle was caught by a speed camera, travelling over the speed limit on the A20." At this point he laid down a photograph taken by the speed camera.

Brett Carson ignored it, but his solicitor moved it closer to them for a better view.

"You can see in this image that you are driving quite close behind," Hammond stated.

"So what? You knew I was driving behind the van because I reported it later on."

Hammond continued his thread, "Just after the van was photographed by the speed camera, the body of a newborn infant was forcibly ejected from the back of the van. You were travelling behind this van, and you reported the death under the name of your employee David Hargreaves."

Brett Carson frowned. "Yes, I admitted that bit."

Hammond leaned forward slightly. "Why?"

Brett Carson looked surprised by the question. "Why? Because a baby had been thrown from the back of a moving van! It's not exactly something that you see every day!"

Hammond nodded slightly. "So, you're saying that the novelty factor of the incident compelled you to report it?"

"No! I mean it was a crime that had to be reported! I only used a different name because I didn't want to be implicated in the death of a newborn baby!"

"I agree that seems the more plausible reason, Mr Carson. However, my suggestion is that the only reason you reported it was because you knew there was a chance that you would have been clocked by the speed camera travelling behind a van that was transporting illegally trafficked passengers. You knew, because you had supervised the handover from Kai Masters and were following behind the van to supervise the delivery. I also suggest that the only reason you stopped the car and reported the death of the baby was because you needed to divert attention from your connection with Kai Masters. The baby's birth had not been expected – at least, not during transit."

"The baby had been thrown from the van in an act of panic; its unexpected arrival could cause delay, it was a complication better to be disposed of. The roads were quiet, there were no witnesses, so the baby would have been reported and subsequently forgotten as an abandoned infant."

There was silence.

Hammond continued, "Tymek Mural was the driver of the hire vehicle. He has admitted to being involved in the transportation of trafficked migrants. He has also admitted that he dumped the body of the newborn's mother after she had died from postpartum haemorrhage. Furthermore, Mr Carson, he has made a sworn statement that he acted under your orders."

"I don't even know anyone called Tymek. Why would he say that I ordered him to do it? The man is delusional!"

Hammond shrugged. "According to Tymek Mural, he had been employed by you as a delivery driver (his words, not mine). His role was to meet Kai Masters at pre-arranged venues. Masters would hand over the passengers and then Tymek would drive them to any given destination. In his statement, he has sworn that you would give him the venues and the times where he was to meet Masters for the collection, and where he was to deliver."

Brett Carson's jaw was tense, but otherwise his body was well controlled. He simply shook his head.

"Do you deny this?"

"Yes."

"Do you deny that you have ever employed Tymek Mural as a driver?"

"Yes."

"Can you explain why your fingerprints were found on a small bundle of false identification cards willingly submitted to us by Mr Mural which we know you handed him during your last meeting?"

Brett Carson swallowed, playing for time. His eyes flicked towards his solicitor before returning to meet Hammond's gaze. Deciding to call the detective's bluff, he stated a simple, "No."

"Do you deny that you have worked with Kai Masters?"

"Yes."

At this point, Hammond's gaze left Carson's face. He looked down and selected a page from the pile before him.

"This is a mobile phone call log used by Tymek Mural. It shows that he called your work mobile at 06.36 on the 18th August. The call lasted five minutes. In his statement, Tymek has said that he called you when the baby had been born, asking you what he should do. You ordered him to get rid of the baby. The fact that there is logged communication between you is adequate evidence that you know him."

Hammond retrieved another item from the pile – a small notebook that was sealed inside a plastic envelope. He laid it down on the table in front of Carson. Then he selected photographs of the same notebook, but the pages had been opened showing the details inside.

"This notebook belongs to Kai Masters. The book has been marked into columns. There are dates, times, and records of cash transactions next to initials. In particular, I am interested in showing you the entries with the initials B.C. written next to them."

"They are not my initials."

"I think they are, Mr Carson. The amounts shown next to the initials will match up with withdrawals made from your business accounts. In addition, one of those dates include the 18th August. The time beside it shows when the tide was low. I believe that if we were to go through each date and time of low tide listed in this book, we may be able to connect not only your financial outgoings but would be able to find a pattern with your incoming transactions as well."

"Which would prove what exactly?"

"We suspect that it would act as supporting evidence that not only did you arrange to have illegal migrants brought over for the intention of selling them as cheap labour, but that you had invested in Kai Master's operation."

Brett Carson began whispering to his solicitor. Hammond waited.

Eventually Carson turned back to the detective. "You have nothing other than a few scribbles on paper and a statement from someone I don't know."

"Mr Carson. In addition to these items of evidence, we have a statement from Bradley Kelsey. He was your former supplier of migrant workers, and he is willing to testify that in court. We have evidence that you were acquainted with Mr Kelsey due to financial transactions you have made in the past. Tymek Mural worked for Nigel Berwick in his industrial waste works. According to Bradley Kelsey, you had employed migrant workers because they were more tolerant to working with toxic substances in your pigment manufacturing company. Kai Masters had an arrangement to dispose of your toxic waste at the same industrial waste works where Tymek worked."

Hammond paused, sighed, and opened his hands, palm up.

"You have to admit," he said, "it all adds up to lots of coincidences."

*

"He's right of course" DCI Hunt remarked to Hammond as they clinked coffee mugs later in mutual congratulation. "A jury may think the whole case against the Carson Brothers is built on conjecture."

Hammond smirked into his drink. "I thought it was about making arrests and charges, not convictions."

DCI Hunt noted the sarcasm but ignored it. "Either way, we've done our job. We've got results."

Edwards leaned against the table. "We haven't found the remaining migrants. They could be passed from one place to another and we wouldn't be able to stop it. It leaves a bad taste in my mouth."

Hammond sympathised. "It's out of our hands now."

Edwards discarded his coffee and left the room. Hammond sympathised with the despondency of his colleague, but experience had shown him that not all questions could be granted answers.

DCI Hunt watched Edwards' haughty departure. He nudged Hammond's shoulder and leaned his head down so he could talk discreetly. "I have some news on one of the unidentified victims from the beach. The intelligence gathered from the French warehouse gave some clues, although nothing that could be used as evidence in prosecution. I just thought you may be interested."

Hammond expressed his interest with a raised chin. "I am."

"I will make sure you receive it." DCI Hunt offered a faint smile. "I have many regrets about this case," he said.

Hammond nodded. "We made too many mistakes."

"No, I mean, I did wrong. I always thought of the victims as no more than evidence. I never considered them as having been people with lives of their own. I realise I have done the same every time I have referred to them as migrants or immigrants. I did not acknowledge them as refugees."

"It's a word," said Hammond. "It's probably down to language."

"No, I mean I did not consider them to have had a reason to seek refuge. I did not recognise them for what they were – people who were desperate to survive. Of course, the stories are there; I have read them and listened to them, but after a while you become numb to the emotion. This case has reawakened the need in me to understand what makes people so desperate they will climb through barbed wire, risk their lives crossing perilous oceans, walk thousands of miles to alien countries. It is simply luck that separates us from those refugees. That realisation has humbled me."

Hammond contemplated Hunt's words. "Then it has had a positive result," he said.

"You'll receive an e-mail updating you on the postmortem reports on the body found with Kai's at Elm Cottage. It has been confirmed as his mother. It looks as if she died after being hit with a blunt instrument to the side of the head."

Hammond thanked his for the update.

"Ironically, Kai means forgiveness in Japanese," Hunt mused aloud. He turned and offered his hand to Hammond in a farewell gesture. "It has been a pleasure working with you."

Hammond didn't reply, but simply smiled and eased his hand back.

CHAPTER TWENTY-TWO

Wallace Hammond was in awe. The woman he had married 27 years before looked more beautiful than he had ever seen her. Lyn was radiating happiness, and despite knowing it wasn't his presence that made her light up, it was the most wonderful sight Wallace had seen in a long time.

There was no sadness or envy when he approached Cameron to shake his hand and congratulate him on his nuptials. Instead, there was a new-found respect for a man who had caused Lyn to be so happy. She was, and would remain, one of the most precious people in his life, but now he had to let go. Although, Hammond insisted, it was only fair he should have one last dance with her.

She had laughed and commented on the fact she didn't have protective boots on, but allowed him to take her over to the dance floor anyway. He swayed awkwardly in the middle of the floor with Lyn held against him until the music stopped.

"Thank you," she said, before returning to her husband at the head table.

Hammond stood at the side of the dance floor looking for Paul. His eyes scanned inside the marquee where guests were now selecting from a choice of cold meats and salads. His gaze paused whilst he registered an attractive woman standing by the piano smiling for his attention. He waved and smiled shyly before registering Paul at the bar.

"It's been a successful day." Hammond eased into conversation with his son.

Paul nodded, but was more occupied with downing the pint glass. "Yep, Mum is happy," he said.

Hammond smiled and slapped his son on the back. "So, is it you and Bettina getting hitched next?" He used a light tone, hoping to disguise his genuine curiosity.

"Hell, no, I'm too young for all that yet!" Paul laughed and offered his father a drink from the bar.

Hammond ordered a whisky. He toasted the happiness of his son and his ex-wife, and downed the contents of the glass in one gulp.

EPILOGUE

October arrived with a burst of sunshine. The air had a crispness that was fresh and invigorating. Hammond drank in the atmosphere from his open window. He surveyed the town below him and considered whether it was time to move on. The thought appealed to him, and he retrieved the laptop from the living room with the intention of looking up property prices. He reckoned there would be enough in his account to put towards a two-bedroom flat; maybe Paul could stay over sometimes.

He had plugged in the laptop and was waiting for the start-up screen to appear, when he was disturbed by his door buzzer. He had a delivery. It was unexpected, and therefore a welcomed surprise. He signed receipt of delivery, shut the door with his foot, and studied the padded envelope before ripping it open. Inside were several typed pages, bound together, and a Post-It note stuck on top.

The translation was a bit slower than I expected but I hope you now have one of the answers you seek. Stay humble. Best regards, Xavier Hunt

Hammond peeled off the Post-It note. At the top of the page, he read:

Translation from Dari into English

Diary Entry found in Warehouse at

The words beside it had been covered in layers of black pen.

Translator: The words beside the entry were also blacked out. Beside it, in red pen, there was a scribbled note. *(Translator's identity has been protected.)*

Diary entry of male identified as Omaid.

He had dreamt of the wolves again. The same scene replayed itself in his mind night after night and was interrupted only by the thoughts of his family. Then he would awake and remember the journey he had survived, and it gave him strength to continue, for he knew that his troubles would soon cease to exist. Soon he would be given a new home, a new life that eventually he could share with those he loved most. Time meant nothing to him any more, but he knew it had been 12 years since the Muslim fundamentalists had taken his father, a pure Afghan who had fought the Russians. For ten years his father had been the patriotic brother who had believed in his country, had been willing to give up his life for his nation, only to be taken away as a traitor long after the Russians had left. It was three years since his mother had sold their land in Ningarhar to pay for her only son to find sanctuary after he had refused to fight his Afghan brothers. Mother had been afraid; she had lost her husband, she could not allow her son to be lost as well. He had helped her gather as many belongings as she could, had taken his weeping sisters by the hands, and accompanied them to Pakistan before the last embrace. His mother had pressed what money she had into his hand and begged him not to forget her, to return home and collect his sisters when he could. Then she had pressed her hand to his cheek and bid him safe passage. The pain he had felt since convinced him he had left his heart with her. In Pakistan, he met the men who would travel with him. They travelled by bus on the rough route from Peshawar south through Quetta and then east through Iran, until they disembarked at Tabriz, met up with their smuggler, and ventured through rocky tracks up to the mountains. The snow had piled so high it was hard to lift their feet, but they had continued, sometimes dragging one another, sometimes pushing. His legs had burned with every step and he had cried in desperation, cried for his mother, for his sisters, and for his father's soul, until the men had threatened to beat him if he did not keep quiet. So he had bitten his tongue and prayed silently. They had walked for many hours when they found the bodies of their predecessors; Five desperates who had attempted to shelter amongst the rocks. They were wedged so tightly together that they had frozen as a mass of entwined limbs. Hazrat, a fellow refugee, had sunk to his knees. He kissed the snow, the rocks, and opened his arms to the sky above him, and his companions repeated his actions. Together, they had washed the feet of their deceased brothers with the snow. They cleansed themselves and prayed Janazah. They wrapped the bodies with any white material they could find amongst their supplies, and packed the snow around them to ensure their safe keeping on their journey back to Allah. Those who Allah had created, Allah would reclaim as his faithful servants, for he and the men had granted them intercession.

The mountain had refused to allow them safe passage without claiming another from his party, and on the third day in the mountains, they were seen by soldiers who started shooting at them. Their smuggler ran off. Gulwari was shot in the leg; they knew he could not walk another step. He had kissed them and bid them farewell.

It was two weeks before they arrived at their destination. Here, they had waited with the hope that the promise to collect them would be fulfilled. They had no idea how long they would have to wait. Shelter was found amongst the largest rocks that overlooked the farm down in the valley below. From here, they snacked on dates and shared the water they had collected from the melted snow. Then the wolves had come.

The wolves had been hungry. The snow had made hunting difficult for them. They had been scouting the farm. The largest of the pack had tried to lure the farm dog away from the farm where the pack were waiting to pounce, but then they saw the men who were so weak they were practically defenseless. An easy kill.

For many long hours, the wolves watched them at a distance, circling around their prey and then drawing closer. The men had collected sticks and stones ready for the attack, but when it came, they were unprepared. The alpha had launched himself with teeth bared, and brought the men down, ripping them, tearing at their flesh.

His memories were fearful. They caused the sweat to run down from his face. His hands and back were clammy. He was shaking, whimpering. Just like he did every morning when he awoke, he slapped his forehead to beat the image from his mind. The image of crimson snow.

The guilt he carried with him was all-consuming; he had run away, leaving the men to their fate, down towards the farm, expecting the wolves to chase him, but for some merciful reason they had not.

The farm had been an unwelcoming and dangerous shelter. He had known that if he was found he would be sold or killed, but he had stayed long enough to steal the food that had been left out for the dog. Silently, he had appealed to his mother, asking for her forgiveness and understanding. As a child, she had made him promise never to steal, but that one time he had needed to. He needed to survive so he could return to her.

The farmer found him and sold him to another smuggler who put him in a truck secretly fitted with seats in oil tankers. There were other passengers, but no-one spoke, each too occupied with their thoughts *and silent prayers. He did not know where he was bound. The journey was uncomfortable and frightening. In Zeytinburno, he was sold to the police for $500 and moved to a basement sweatshop where he was forced to work 19 hours without break every day for 12 months, sewing sheepskin waistcoats for the bazaar whilst he was chained to the bench on which he sat. One night, when he was close to giving up, he wrote his mother a letter. He told her he loved her, he loved his sisters. He promised he would send them help. He knew as he wrote that they may not be alive, that they may have given up hope, or worse, that they thought he had forgotten them, so he signed the letter with his full name, just in case it was found on his body. He hoped the letter would find its way home.*

The letter was secreted amongst his clothes and he slept a fitful sleep with the resolve to carry on. The thought of his family gave him strength. He continued to work until his debt was paid and he was able to pay for the boat that would take him to Europe.

In summer, he had waited with hundreds in Istanbul, hoping to board the fishing boats bound for Italy. It seemed as if he would never be able to leave, but the love for his mother drove him on and eventually he accepted passage on a faster dinghy from the Albanian Scafisti. There were about 20 other refugees with him, including a family of three – a man who held onto the hand of a small child, and a woman who kept her head down at all times. The driver of the boat had not looked at his passengers once. They were guarded by another Albanian who constantly watched them and the waters to check for the police.

The journey had been quick; they were told they would arrive in Italy within two hours of leaving Istanbul. For the first time in many months, his heart had lifted with joy at the thought that his journey was almost complete. But his travel to Italy ended quicker than anticipated. He had been occupied with watching the coastline, hoping for a first glimpse of the Italian horizon, when the boat suddenly swerved with such force he was thrown towards the feet of his guard. Bewildered, he looked up from the footwell just in time to see the child and her father fall into the water. Instantly, another passenger had thrown himself after the man and child, in a desperate attempt to save them. Fear had pinned him to the floor of the boat. He had covered his head with his arms in terror, hearing the constant screams and wailing of the mother who now had knelt to her knees, gripping the trousers of the guard and pleading with him to turn the boat around.

Instead, the boat picked up speed and slapped over the waves in its desperate attempt to further the distance between itself and the pursuing Italian police boat. Bewildered by the sudden change and the desperate cries around him, he had lifted himself to his knees by clinging onto the rope handles at the side of the dinghy, and looked behind them in time to see the pursuing boat slow down to where the figures were floundering in the water. The dinghy sped on.

The same afternoon, he had arrived in Bari. The Afghan community was prepared for him and his fellow passengers, and they managed to get them onto a train bound for Rome, where he was taken to another smuggler. His funds were now almost depleted, but his last dollars paid for the entry into a wholesale depot where trucks were loading cargo bound for Calais. Hidden under crates of cooking oil, he had stayed hidden until the truck stopped. The back doors opened and a voice in French had said, "You can fuck off now. You've reached the Jungle."

AUTHOR'S NOTE

The background of this novel is based on the work of law enforcement officers of Kent Police and the Kent and Essex Serious Crime Directorate. It is a work of fiction that has been loosely based on procedures and investigation, but it is not intended to portray realistic events or investigations that have taken place in Kent Police's history.

The novel was written between 2012 and 2013, when economic migration was considered to be the biggest threat to the stability of British civilisation. Just over a year later, Europe faced the biggest refugee crisis since the Second World War. The majority of those desperate to reach Europe were not only escaping poverty, but war, dictatorial oppression, and religious extremism.

There has been the intention to imitate experiences of some who have attempted to seek refuge in Great Britain, although this is a work of fiction so the names of characters, places, and timing are not authentic.

C. D. Neill
September 2015

www.ingramcontent.com/pod-product-compliance
Lightning Source LLC
Chambersburg PA
CBHW030306200626
46816CB00002BA/785